OH FUCK
OH FUCK
IT HURTS

A COLLECTION OF MEDICAL HORROR

BY RUTH ANNA EVANS
WITH GUEST AUTHOR RIK HOSKIN

WWW.RUTHANNAEVANS.COM

CONTENTS

CONTENT WARNINGS

MAY CONTAIN SPOILERS

All stories contain some level of medical trauma

FAT: Fatphobia, internalized fatphobia, self-mutilation

Defective: Traumatic childbirth, infant suffering and death

Colonoscopy: Feces

Side Effects Include: Suicidality

INTRODUCTION

PAIN. IT CAN BE sharp, a needle jammed into your vein by an uncaring tech. It can be twisting, a cramp squeezing a clot of blood from your uterus or a baby from your womb. It can be splitting, a migraine that cuts your head in two. But always, always, with pain comes fear. And where there is fear, there is horror.

This book is about the fear and suffering that comes when our bodies betray us, and betray us they will. At any moment, any of us could have a lump of blood hit the wrong organ and find ourselves forever trapped in a breathing corpse, not aware enough to wish for death. We could get Covid, and then long Covid, and then be chronically ill for the rest of our lives.

We could give birth, as the mother in *Defective* does, to a baby so wrong it in itself is a betrayal. Or we could simply start going bald at the age of forty, watching ourselves in the mirror as we age, nothing to be done.

Some of us are lucky with good health, lousy with luck in that regard, though death comes to us all. Others of us always seem to draw the short straw. I personally fall somewhere in the middle. I was physically healthy until the birth of my child, though I've had bipolar since my late teens. But shortly after childbirth, I experienced an autoimmune cascade in which I developed Hashimoto's and Ulcerative Colitis. Those two diagnoses have left me more than once on the verge of disability, unable to make it through a day of work, unable to care for my family. I am so incredibly grateful for the tens of thousands of dollars worth of medication that I take each month. These medications allow me to work, and parent, and live my life with manageable symptoms. I recognize that access to this health care is a privilege, and if you lack this access, my heart is with you.

Even well-managed chronic illness comes with a large helping of fear, though. I'm afraid that the injection I give myself to keep my colon from developing bleeding ulcers will stop working, or that the insurance company will change some line-item and that it will be stolen away. I am afraid that my medications will cause heart problems, cancer, more weight gain. I'm afraid these headaches are something worse, something new. All possible, all r eal.

You'll see my fears in these stories, from the real-life flash, *Colonoscopy* to the bizarre short, *FAT.*

About *FAT.* My diseases and their accompanying medications have left me obese. It sucks. We live in a world that expects fat people to voluntarily torture themselves. My story about what it's like to live in a fat, medicalized body is one of my favorites in this collection. If you have weight issues, though, it's filled with triggers, so proceed with caution.

The horrors in this book came from my experiences with disability, my pain, and my fear.

When I decided to publish it, I felt the need for a balancing voice, so that it wasn't all navel-gazing. I opened up a submission call, and found what I hope you'll agree is a story that strengthens this collection with another perspective. Author Rik Hoskin has a stunningly clear voice and his story, with its masterful twist, is one I am proud to include in this book. I hope you enjoy it as much as I did.

Thank you for reading this book. Thank you for opening yourself to such painful stories. Writing them gave me some relief from my own pain and fear, and I hope that they bring you some relief of your own.

LIFELINE

"DID YOU FIND THE wallet?"

"Not yet."

"Well, goddammit, find the wallet!" Jane pumped on the unconscious man's chest with all of her one hundred and forty pounds.

"Found it!" Jeremy pulled a black leather billfold from the laptop bag he had been digging through. The Starbucks patrons standing around staring all visibly relaxed a tiny bit.

"Stick it in the slot, dumbass!" Jane never had much of a filter at times like these. Jeremy always let it go. He firmly slid the Mastercard into the AED machine, which flashed to life. Jane had already cut off the man's shirt and quickly shaved his chest. She attached the AED pads and hit the button. The machine counted down, then called for all clear and provided a jolt. Everyone waited with held breath. The machine detected a rhythm.

The numbers on the credit card reader spun.

Jane leaned back and wiped the sweat from her forehead. Jeremy tried to give her a high-five, but she just looked at him, exhausted. He grinned.

"Let's get him loaded up. I'll monitor him; you drive and call ahead to let them know we're coming," Jane said.

The paramedics got the man—Vinnie, his credit card said—hoisted into the back of the ambulance and headed to the hospital.

"How's he doing?" Jeremy called back.

"Looks like he hasn't hit his limit yet," Jane replied, watching the numbers rack up.

"Is there another card, in case?"

"There's one more. Looks like a debit card, though."

"That won't last long."

"Nope."

"Blue card?"

"No."

They arrived at the hospital and a nurse was waiting at the door, card reader held out. Jane swiftly switched the Mastercard from the ambulance's machine to the hospitals. She had become a pro at this. Jeremy handed over the man's wallet and gave the field report.

"Unconscious when we arrived. Bystanders reported that he clutched his chest and collapsed. He was down completely for maybe ten minutes. We were nearby but it took a minute to find the wallet."

The nurse, Cassie, nodded. "More people need to get the credit implant. Safer that way." Jane managed not to roll her eyes. The implant cost thousands.

Vinnie remained unconscious, though the machines said his heart was beating. Jane and Jeremy headed back out on their shift and Cassie rolled Vinnie back to a bay.

He didn't wake. Cassie entered the code for a doctor's consult, which in the emergency room was $7,223, and waited, tense, while the machine ran the card. It was approved.

The doctor came quickly. An efficient, humorless man, he directed Cassie on which medications to begin to support the man's heart, and ordered a series of tests.

"Credit limit?" he asked before leaving.

"Unknown," Cassie answered. "No blue card, either."

The doctor made a face.

It was halfway through the coronary angiogram that the machine beeped. Vinnie's credit limit must have been $15,000. Cassie quickly switched it out for the debit card she had held at the ready.

"Hurry, Margaret, we may not have enough to get a blood thinner in him."

"I know; I'm hurrying," Margaret answered. "Okay, yeah, he's got a clot. Page the doctor."

The doctor answered right away and barked out a prescription and an order for a repeated test in a few hours. Cassie eyed the machine. It was up to $16,500. She always tried not to get too wrapped up in the credit-unknown cases, but it was hard.

"Come on, Vinnie, just a little more."

She was about to inject the medication when the machine beeped. Cassie searched the wallet again, knowing that it was empty.

"I'm sorry, Vinnie," she said, laying her hand on his chest briefly before returning the medication to the cabinet, glad she hadn't punctured the top of the vial and had to throw it away.

Cassie went to the nurse's station and found the nursing assistant.

"Suze, bay four is going to need watching."

The girl, a new assistant, and young, blinked hard.

"Again? I just took one this morning."

"I know. I'm sorry. He hit his limit."

"Okay."

Suze walked slowly into Vinnie's bay and stood witness while he breathed raggedly. It wasn't long before he went rigid. If he had been wearing a heart monitor, it would have shown a flatline, but those weren't pro bono anymore. All that was provided was the watcher.

After his body relaxed, Suze waited a moment and then took his pulse. Nothing.

She poked her head out.

"Gone," she told Cassie.

Cassie nodded. They avoided each other's eyes, as was customary for this part.

"Move him out," Cassie said, after a moment. "We need the bay."

AUTOIMMUNE

IT WAS HAPPENING AGAIN. That small itch that wouldn't go away. And when Gio twisted to look in the mirror in the employee bathroom, there was the tell-tale mottled redness. It was tucked deep into an old scar, but he was sure. Soon, his whole body would be on fire with a deep, painful itch, one for which there really ought to be another word. And then...he couldn't think about the next stage.

The specialists' urgent care was open until seven, but he was scheduled to work until eight. He radioed the manager, Neil, who was probably sitting on his ass in the office. But Neil hated it when associates came in, and Gio didn't want to piss him off right before asking to leave.

"Hey, boss, looks like I need to head out a couple of hours early if that's okay." Gio kept his voice light. "Got to swing by the doctor's office, get something checked out."

Another benefit of asking for decency over the radio was that everyone would be able to hear it if Neil decided to be a dick.

There was no response at first, then a curt, "Fine. Make sure you finish your section."

"Thank you!" Gio clipped back, trying to sound appreciative but refusing to suck up. He went back to the toilet paper aisle and finished the price changes. They were all going up, of course. People would bitch at him about that, just like they bitched about everything.

· · · · ● ● ● ● ● · ·

A tired-looking nurse practitioner examined the spot on his back and as expected ordered a patch test.

"It's not eczema," Gio said. "It's never eczema. It's a flare."

"We have to check." The man had probably had this conversation with ten people today.

"Is there anything new to try?"

"Let's try the high-dose steroids first."

"They don't work."

"The insurance company says we have to try them."

"What's after that this time?"

"There's a trial you'll be eligible for if you fail steroids again. Make an appointment for two weeks and if there's no improvement we'll talk about the trial."

Two weeks. He had to let this thing develop for two weeks. He knew exactly what shape he would be in by then.

·· • • • • • • ··

The scraping for the patch test hurt, as it always did. He didn't flinch. How many times had he done this now? Too many to count. At least this tech was quick.

·· • • • • • • ··

The next morning, the itch was bone-deep. The splitting had started on his calves and ribcage, his skin opening in sharp seams, glistening white flesh exposed like the fat on a steak, deeper red peeking through beneath. And the seeping had begun.

He had a shift. He couldn't call in yet. It was going to get worse, and he needed to save his days.

Wrapping his wounds tightly with bandages and then medical tape and then more bandages, he let a few tears leak out. He always allowed himself to cry once when he started a flare. It was only fair.

· · · ● · ● · · · ·

Work was hell. Lifting and bending tore his flesh until it was screaming. His bandages were soaked after an hour.

Neil caught him leaning against a shelf, his head in his hands.

"This isn't your house," Neil barked. "Get it together or go home."

"Sorry," Gio mumbled, and grabbed his box knife from his waist, slicing open a box of sponges. He wished he were slicing Neil's face.

· · · · • · • · · ·

Gio was at the stage where he started to see bone. The itching stopped, which was good because when he touched his skin it came off in his hands. His face had a rip down one side, and his knuckles were splitting, too, joints peering out like little white eggs. Two more days before he could return to the doctor with proof the steroids weren't working.

He had a shift.

· · · · • · • · · ·

"What the hell is wrong with your skin?" Neil stared at him in the toothpaste aisle, like it was Gio's fault his flesh was falling from his skeleton.

"It's an autoimmune condition. I'm receiving treatment."

"Well, you're bleeding on the fucking tooth-paste. Go home."

"I need this shift."

"Go. Home."

· · · •• • • • · · ·

He was in the doctor's office waiting room at eight in the morning on the fourteenth day after his first appointment. He brought a mylar blanket with him to protect the chair from his seepage. The other patients sat far from him. He had started the smelly stage.

The nurse practitioner nodded when he walked into the room.

"Okay. I would agree that the steroids are not effective. Let me tell you about our trial."

Maggots. The treatment was maggots.

"We believe that the maggots work with your immune system to end the flare," the practitioner explained, as though he weren't suggesting covering Gio's body with larvae. "They have to get deep into the tissue to be effective."

"Fine. When can we start?"

"You have to call the procedures office," the practitioner said. "They'll give you the number at check-out."

"How long does it take to schedule?"

"A few days. A week. Not long."

Not long. How much flesh would he lose in those days, that week? He was starting to worry about his cartilage. The doctors never mentioned it but he knew that the disease attacked cartilage-based appendages once it had spread throughout the flesh.

· · · · ● ● · ● ● · · ·

He lost an ear. Woke up in the morning and it was laying on his pillow. Blood oozed from the stump. He grabbed a towel and applied pressure until the bleeding stopped, put the ear in a plastic container and put it in the fridge. Maybe they could reattach it once his skin regrew.

· · · · ● ● · ● ● · · ·

Neil texted. Fired after missing too many shifts. He switched to his credit card for groceries and let his mother know he wouldn't have the rent. She said she was sorry he was sick again and to let her know when he could pay her back.

· · · ● · ● ● · · · ·

They got him in for the maggots two days later. When the tech applied the larvae, they slipped off of his exposed bones.

"It doesn't look like you have enough flesh left for it to work this way," she said, apologetic.

The woman called in the doctor.

"I think we'll have to use the tank," he said, leveling a gaze at Gio. "It's a little extreme. You'll be covered in maggots. Your whole body. Do you think you can handle that?"

Gio nodded. Fine. There was no choice.

They fitted his face with a breathing apparatus. His nose had decayed somewhat but held. He was concerned that the pus from his lips would be trapped and block his breathing, but the device provided suction for that.

They dumped the maggots in by the bucketful. Tiny moving larvae covered his body, tickling, nibbling. They squirmed into him, right next to the bone. Like little grains of rice, wriggling, burrowing.

Please work, he prayed. *You can do it, little guys.*

They left him in the tank for twenty minutes and prescribed twenty minutes a day for two weeks.

They couldn't shower him because his remaining skin would slough off, so they had him stand and let the maggots fall off back into the tank. Then they carefully picked the remaining creatures out of him with tweezers.

He cried again. A two-cry flare was a bad one.

· · · · ● · ● · · · ·

His scars were deep and they couldn't reattach the ear, but the treatment worked.

"Thank you," he said to the nurse practitioner. "I appreciate you getting me into the trial."

"Of course," the NP answered. "I hope it's a while before your next flare."

"You and me both." He managed a smile.

· · · · ●·●· · ·

Neil at first refused to give him his job back.

"You'll scare the customers. You look like shit."

"It's a documented disability."

"So?"

"So you shouldn't have fired me to begin with. I could get a lawyer."

"You can't afford a lawyer."

"There's an organization that provides them."

"Well, fuck me." Neil leaned back in his chair. "Fine. Wear long sleeves and long pants."

"It's hot in the back."

"Do you want this job?"

"Okay."

· · · · ●·●· · ·

Toilet paper prices went up again. He paid his mom back for the rent money. He wore long sleeves and long pants and grew his hair out over the stump where his ear used to be.

Thirteen months later, he felt another itch.

This time, it was a three-cry flare.

FAT

CARA POURED THE CONTENTS of the little silver package into her bowl and mixed in some water, as directed. The packets had just arrived that day, and she had the feeling that always accompanied a new diet—not excitement exactly, but a mix of hope and dread. What if it worked? What if it failed?

She picked up her fork and forced herself to put the "food" in her mouth. It tasted worse than she expected, and she had expected it to be pretty bad. It was sawdust, after all. They had promised flavors—chicken, beef, basil—but it just tasted like sawdust. All of the moisture was sucked out of her tongue, and she gagged. She clamped her lips shut and forced herself to keep it in her mouth. Finally, the gagging stopped and she swallowed.

A sip of her low-calorie energy drink added the taste of turpentine to the mix but allowed her to choke it down.

It's worth it, she told herself. *Don't be a baby.*

The ads for weight loss never stopped on her social media feeds, and this one had a viral video behind it. The woman had lost fifty pounds in six weeks, and she looked fantastic. For Cara, fifty pounds would barely make a dent, but since she had been gaining again lately, she was willing to try anything. Even sawdust. She took another bite, forcing herself to swallow. Her stomach rumbled, wanting real food. Pizza. Sushi. Hell, even a good salad.

Maybe if you weren't such a fat-ass, the voice in her head told her. It was always there, one thought away. It sounded like her mother with a dash of her last boyfriend. He was gone forty pounds ago. Now she couldn't engage with any of the men who contacted her because she couldn't tell the good guys from the fetishists. She didn't check her direct messages anymore. It was too depressing.

"Mom, that looks awful." Tillie was eight and always told the truth.

"I know," Cara said, taking another bite. "But it's supposed to work."

"They're all supposed to work."

"I know," Cara said again. She dumped the rest of the mess into the trash and washed the grit out of her mouth with water. She couldn't take another drink of the vile energy concoction, no matter how many calories it was supposed to burn.

She felt her gut rumble. She had wondered if that part of the miracle sawdust would live up to the hype. It was supposed to "bond" with the fat in your digestive system and fast-track it out before it had a chance to make itself at home.

"I'm going to be in the bathroom for a bit, sweetie," she told Tillie. "Can you put on a video?"

"Sure." Tillie looked at her mom a little sideways. "Are you okay?"

"I'm fine, just gotta let this thing work."

Her daughter knew—had always known, really—that Cara was trying to lose weight. When she was younger, she tried to convince her mother to eat with her, holding her chicken nuggets and apple slices to her mother's lips. Cara would be so hungry, but she'd never take a bite. Tillie had given up, but she was always curious about the next, usually disgusting, fad. Once, she snuck into the fridge and stole one of Cara's chocolate shakes designed to make you throw up after eating. She had been sick for two days. Cara still hadn't forgiven herself for that. Since then, she kept her special foods locked up, but it seemed Tillie had learned her lesson.

Cara settled onto the toilet and prepared to suffer. It seemed like most of her life was a boomerang between starving and suffering. There had to be something else she could do.

A part of her wanted to give up, to just be fat, to accept it and move on and try to be happy about things other than her body. But she was too fat for that. Her body was nothing but bulges. Sitting with her pants down made her feel sick, and not from the disgusting food. Her abdomen was a map of old and new stretch marks, as her skin had unstitched itself to make room for each new pound.

Her doctor couldn't tell her why she gained weight like she did, didn't bother to investigate. They always just told her to diet and exercise, but she knew—she KNEW—she didn't eat more or sit around more than her normal-weight friends. Back when she had friends. It wasn't fair. And she couldn't keep eating sawdust.

· · · · ·· · · · ·

Cara hated the doctor's office, in huge part because of the scale. She always tried to look away, but she always failed. The nurses were all different in how they handled the weighing-in of a fat person. Today, she had the grimly silent type, who didn't attempt any light conversation while the digital scale adjusted to Cara's heft. She just jotted down the numbers, gave Cara a nod, and led the way to the room. That type was easier than the chatters.

While she waited for the doctor, Cara gave herself a talking-to. She wasn't going to leave this time without a solution. A real solution. Not sawdust.

Not "diet and exercise." Something that would work. This was ridiculous.

There was a little knock on the door and her doctor came in, smiling. As she did with every woman, Cara analyzed her weight, comparing it to her own. She had chosen this doctor because she was an overweight woman—not as overweight as Cara, but still nice and round—so Cara hoped she wouldn't blame her for gaining like the skinny-minis always did. So far, so good. She never even mentioned it.

"How are you today?" Dr. Cox asked.

"Hungry," Cara said. "Always hungry."

"How much are you eating?"

"Hardly at all, really. I just started a new diet."

"Any luck?"

"No. If anything, the opposite."

"I'm sorry." The doctor waited, letting Cara take her time.

"Is there anything medical we can do?" She hadn't asked before because it felt like giving up, like cheating. She couldn't meet the other woman's eyes, and she felt her cheeks flush red.

Except for her daughter, who saw everything with her sharp little eyes, she hadn't talked to another person about her weight in a very long time. Not since she hit 3X. That was when people discreetly stopped talking about their own weight issues around her, stopped dropping mentions of their gym memberships and inviting her. She had moved out of the regular-fat category and into the big-fat category. People assumed at that point that a woman had given up.

"There are a few options," the doctor said. "Some of them are mild and likely ineffective. Some of them are highly effective and quite unpleasant."

"None of them mild and highly effective?" She meant it as a joke, but it came out flat.

"I'm afraid not. There is oral medication we can try, but it's not good for the heart and usually the weight loss is not sustained. Our first step would probably be injections."

"That doesn't sound TOO bad," Cara said hopefully.

"The injections have to go in your bone."

Cara's eyebrows shot up and her jaw dropped. "Your bone?"

"Yes, ma'am. Your hip bone. Right into the marrow."

Cara didn't know what to say.

"And insurance doesn't cover it."

"How much does it cost?"

"The injection itself is $10,000, but you only do it once."

"Once?"

"Once. It works or it doesn't. A lot of times it works."

"How much could I lose?"

"Well. All of it."

"Excuse me?"

"You lose all of the fat in your body."

What?

"Isn't that...isn't that dangerous?"

"Very."

"But people do this?"

"All the time."

"It doesn't, like, kill you?"

"Most of the time, no."

"Most of the time."

"Right."

Cara sat and absorbed the information. A shot that went into her bone marrow and would eliminate all of the fat in her body. This was a real thing?

"What are my other options?"

"Surgery."

"What kind of surgery?"

"Stomach removal."

"Stomach REMOVAL?"

"Yes."

"Not, like, gastric bypass or something?"

"They've found the weight often comes back and people have a hard time not eating too much, which causes serious problems. Without a stomach, you just don't eat, and that problem is solved."

"Don't you...die?"

"You do IV nutrition. Every day."

"Every day."

"Yes."

"Oh. And people do this."

"All the time."

"Do I weigh enough to qualify?"

"Yes. By a good margin."

Cara winced. Ouch.

"To be fair, you don't have to be that over-weight. Some people do it prophylactically."

"You're kidding."

"No."

"Do I have any other options?"

"Stay overweight. You are healthy otherwise. Your risk factors for certain diseases are higher, but so far cholesterol, sugar, blood pressure, it's all fine."

Cara looked at the doctor and saw her face was completely neutral, as though she recognized that none of the options she had presented to Cara were good ones, and she didn't want to sway her in any direction. Cara didn't know what to do. She couldn't do anything that could kill her. She had a daughter. But the idea of being a normal weight…skinny even…

"I'll have to think about it," she said. "There are diets I haven't tried. Maybe I could get a tread-mill."

The doctor nodded and moved on, tapping Cara's knee and making her leg jump. Cara only half-noticed. On her way out of the office, she threw her visit summary in the garbage without looking at it. She didn't have to look to know that it said the same thing it always did. The same thing it always would, if she didn't do something drastic. "Morbidly obese."

· · · · · ● · ● · · ·

Cara was picking Tillie up from school. She scrolled through her phone while the kids streamed out of the low brick building. She'd always felt that the school looked like a prison. It made her sad to drop Tillie off there every morning and happy to pick her up. Tillie never talked much about school.

She spotted her daughter, whose backpack had a rolled-up posterboard sticking out the top. Great. Another project.

"Hey Tillie!" she heard a voice shout. "Why is your mom so fat?"

Tillie locked eyes with her mother, horror on her face. Cara burned with shame as Tillie ducked her head and ran for the car.

"Is that why you're fat too?" the evil child continued. Cara scanned the crowd of children but couldn't find the speaker. She wanted to punch the kid in his horrible face. Tillie threw the car door open and dived in. Tears were running down her cheeks.

"I'm so sorry, honey," Cara said. Tillie turned her head and looked out the window. She didn't say a word the whole way home. When they got home, Tillie went to her room and quietly shut her door behind her. Cara could hear her stifled crying through the door, like a little puppy looking for its mother. Cara wanted to go to her and hold her, but she was ashamed. She told herself her daughter wanted to be left alone, though she knew it wasn't true. What she wanted, Cara couldn't help but think, was a mother who wasn't fat.

· · · ● ● · ● ● · · ·

Cara called to make the appointment first thing the next morning after dropping Tillie off at that hateful place. The $10,000 would drain her entire savings account. She had been hoping to take Tillie on a vacation this summer where they went to all the theme parks they could stomach, but who was she kidding? She wouldn't be able to ride any of the rides anyway. And she didn't want to be seen in public with her daughter right now, for fear her shame would rub off on the little girl more than it had.

The clinic had an opening, it so happened, the following day.

Sitting in her car outside the building, Cara tried not to cry, tried not to blast herself for every potato chip or piece of chocolate she'd ever allowed past her lips.

She was frightened. Her hands trembled as she got out of her car and she dropped her keys. Bending to pick them up, she imagined the whole world staring at her broad backside, nodding their heads and agreeing, yes, it was time to do something about this problem.

She forced herself to approach the reception desk, where a tiny blonde girl cheerfully greeted her.

"And who are you here to see?"

Cara had already forgotten the name of the doctor.

"Nevermind, that's okay, what's your name?"

"Cara Berger." She hated saying her last name.

"Wonderful! Okay, you are seeing Dr. Mantis. Have a seat and we'll get you back there shortly!" The exclamation points in everything the woman said made Cara cringe. This was all just...a lot.

The doctor was a man, middle-aged and handsome. Sprinkles of silver at his temples, no spare tire around his midsection. And he had a warm smile, with kind eyes.

"I've reviewed your chart, Cara, and you are an excellent candidate for Bentiga." The pounding of Cara's heart let up a little. Her blood pressure had been high when the nurse took it, but it was always high with those stupid electronic cuffs. They never fit her arm, even when they used the big-person cuff. And undressing and putting on the paper gown over her bulk always made her extra nervous. But she had also been anxious that she would be met with a 'no'. After finally forcing herself to this appointment, she didn't want to be turned away. So, she was relieved that didn't seem to be happening.

"Can I get the shot today?"

"I don't see why not—that's why you're here, right?"

"Yes."

"Do you have any questions?"

"How long does it take to lose the weight?"

"The medication attacks and dissolves the fat in your body. It will begin working immediately. You should be down about twenty pounds in the first few days, and the weight loss will accelerate after that."

"That sounds...dramatic."

"Yes."

"Are there any side effects I should be aware of?"

"Dizziness. Vomiting. Diarrhea. Migraine. There's the possibility of serious dehydration as the weight comes off. And, it's not really a side effect, but there is the matter of the skin."

"Skin?"

"When you are obese and lose a dramatic amount of weight, there is always excess skin left behind. It is a bother to some people."

Cara thought to herself that if the world would stop using that hateful word about her, then she would be able to live with some extra skin. It couldn't be worse, right?

"There is surgery we can do to remove it, but most insurances don't cover it, and you have to wait until you've lost a certain amount of weight. Some people never get there."

"Why not?"

The doctor paused.

"Why not?" Cara repeated.

"They die."

Cara's heart began its hammering again. There was no one to care for her child if she was gone. But the look on Tillie's face when the mean kid had yelled at her flashed back into her mind's eye.

"What's the mortality rate?"

"Ten percent."

"That seems high."

"Are you a smoker?"

"No." The nurse had asked her these questions.

"Not even once in a while?"

"Never have; it's disgusting."

"Any family history of heart disease?"

"No."

"Autoimmune? Lupus? Fibromyalgia?"

"No, not that I know of."

"You should be okay. I can't tell you for certain, but most people find the risk worth the reward."

Cara nodded. "Okay."

"The only other thing is the pain with injection."

"How much pain?"

"A lot."

Cara had always handled pain fairly well. She thought she'd be okay.

"I'm ready."

As if on cue, there was a little knock on the door and an older woman with a firm look to her popped her head in the room.

"We good to go in here?"

"Come on in—it sounds like the decision has been made," Dr. Mantis said. "Cara, this is Judy, she will be assisting me today."

The woman carried a long white case. Very long. She set it on the counter and snapped the lid open. Inside was a needle that had to be twelve inches. Cara's eyes widened. The tip of the needle glinted, impossibly sharp.

"That's going in my bone?"

"Yes, ma'am. It's made of the strongest metal on the planet. It'll pierce right through."

"Will you numb me at all?"

"We can numb your skin if you like, but the real pain is in the bone itself, and there is nothing to be done about that."

"Can you sedate me?"

"Certainly," the doctor said, but the nurse gave her a little shake of her head.

"It's expensive," Judy said. "Insurance doesn't—"

"Insurance doesn't cover it. Of course. No. Go ahead."

Judy lifted the needle from its case. It shone under the fluorescent lights.

"If you want to move your gown aside, this has to go into your hip," Dr. Mantis said, taking the needle from the nurse.

Cara exposed her pale thigh.

"Higher," Judy said, and Cara complied, biting her lip with embarrassment. Judy just swabbed a spot with an alcohol wipe and moved to the side. "Ready?" She looked Cara dead in the eyes, and Cara almost thought she saw a warning there. She ignored it. She couldn't keep living like this.

"Ready."

The pain was like nothing Cara had ever felt, including the ten minutes prior to her epidural with Tillie. It was like a fiery explosion in her hip bone, like a drill boring into her deepest, tenderest part. She gasped and then gasped again, trying to catch her breath through the pain.

"Almost there, sweetie," Judy said, patting her hand. Cara grabbed the woman's fingers and squeezed, a tear rolling down her face.

"Try not to move," Dr. Mantis said. "We need to get it all in there."

Cara groaned through gritted teeth, forcing herself to stay still. How much longer?

Finally, Dr. Mantis withdrew the needle, and Judy moved to put pressure on the injection site. Cara was full-on sobbing. Her hip felt like it had been broken clean in half.

"Why does it still hurt so much?" she whimpered in a voice that didn't sound like her own. "Will it stop?"

"It takes about an hour for the pain to subside."

"An *hour*?"

Judy handed her two pills and a little cup of water.

"Here is some Tylenol. We'll be back to check on you." The doctor and nurse left. Cara collapsed back on the exam table, feeling like an injured whale. This had better work.

· · · · ● · ● · · ·

It took a little over an hour, but the pain did mostly subside. Judy was back with discharge papers, reminding her of the normal side effects.

"Fever, headache, nausea, diarrhea, all normal," the nurse said. "You just need to call us if you get a fever over 100 degrees."

"What would that mean?"

"A bone infection, most likely."

"That can happen?"

"Yes, though it is not typical."

"And the weight will start coming off right away?"

"You'll see significant weight loss within a day or two," the nurse repeated the doctor's answer to her question. "And it will get faster after that."

"Okay, good."

"It's going to be scary," the nurse said softly, as though sharing a secret she shouldn't.

"Scary?"

"You'll be okay. You're healthy. You're in a good age range for this. Don't panic."

"Why would I panic?"

The nurse gave her shoulder a squeeze and opened the door. Cara hefted herself off the exam table and limped out of the room, down the hall, into the elevator. For once, she didn't chide herself for not taking the stairs and burning those extra calories. It was finally going to happen. She was going to lose her weight. Tillie would be so proud.

......

She was sick all night, on the toilet with a trash can in front of her. Tillie kept knocking on the door, calling, "Mommy, are you okay? Mommy?"

Between heaves, Cara would croak back, "I'm fine, baby! I'll be okay. Get yourself a snack and put on a movie." But she could tell her little girl was camped outside the door, listening to her be sick. She tried to be quiet but couldn't. It lasted for hours.

Finally, her stomach settled. She cleaned herself up and opened the bathroom door. Tillie was asleep on the other side, blankie and stuffed animal clutched tight. Exhausted, Cara bent, picked her daughter up, and carried her into her bedroom, settling her onto her bed.

Tillie's eyes opened.

"Are you okay, Mom?"

"I'm fine, you can sleep now."

"I love you."

"I love you too, baby. Good night."

"Night." Tillie smiled and rolled over, already asleep. Cara glanced at the digital clock. Four in the morning. She would need to keep Tillie home from school in the morning. For once, she was glad that she had been fired from her job for not being able to stand all day, because she wouldn't have to call in. Her manager had always been a dick about that. Now that she'd spent the last of her savings, though, the urgency to find a new job was more intense. She'd have to worry about that in the morning. When she was skinny, finding a job would be a lot easier, anyway.

Cara couldn't help herself. She went back to the bathroom and pulled out the scale. She couldn't remember the last time she had lost more than three pounds. Gaining, always gaining. She held her breath as she stepped on.

Thirty pounds. She had lost thirty pounds. Something was wrong with the scale. She couldn't have. It hadn't even been a full day. An alarm bell started going off in her head. The nurse had told her not to panic, and now she knew what she meant. If she lost thirty pounds in a matter of hours, something drastic was happening inside of her body. Something that really might kill her. Ten percent chance. She turned and looked in the bathroom mirror. Yes, she could tell already. Her stomach, the part of her body she hated the most, sagged a little less. She held out her arms. The paunches that swung underneath seemed a little smaller. Despite her exhaustion from the vomiting and the diarrhea and the pain from the shot still lingering, she felt her heart lift. She had tried so long to lose weight. And now, in less than a day, it had happened.

"Thank God," she whispered to herself. "Thank God." There was a sense of alarm creeping beneath the relief, but she shut it out of her mind, blocking it with visions of herself and Tillie on a roller coaster. What would it be like to not worry about whether her daughter would fly to her death because the safety bar had to accommodate Cara's fat body? It had been so long since she hadn't spent most of her time thinking about how much she weighed. It was worth the ten percent chance. It was worth it. She took her night meds and went to bed, excited to see how much more weight she would lose overnight.

· · · ● · ● ● · ● · ·

Cara woke up with a splitting, screaming headache. She stumbled to the bathroom and ran the water cold in the bathtub and stuck her head under the faucet. She vomited and watched through searing eyes as the sick ran down the drain.

She didn't hear Tillie come in, just felt her daughter's hand, rubbing her back. "You're okay, you're okay," she murmured, just as Cara always did for her when she was throwing up. "Do you want me to get you your headache medicine?"

Cara turned her head and washed her mouth out, then shut off the water.

"Just bring me a towel, baby."

Tillie handed her a mostly dry towel and watched silently as Cara squeezed the water out of her hair. Cara's head felt a little better from the cold water and the throwing up.

"I'm sorry I'm sick, sweetie," she said, sitting on the edge of the bathtub. "It won't be forever. It's that shot."

"The one to lose weight?"

"Yes."

"You're skinnier." Tillie said it in a careful, neutral way. "A lot skinnier."

"Really?"

Tillie nodded, her eyes wide.

Cara pushed herself to her feet and went to the scale, still dripping a little. She accounted for the weight of the water in her clothes and hair, doing that mental subtraction all women do when being weighed. Five pounds for shoes if you left them on, five pounds for clothes, ten for a sweater. But the number on the scale didn't require any subtraction. Cara's hand flew to her mouth and she gasped. She was sixty pounds down from her original weight. She had lost another thirty pounds while she had been sleeping. Tears of joy sprang to her eyes. It was working. She wasn't going to be fat anymore.

Another wave of nausea hit her and she scrambled to make it to the toilet, heaving up bile. Even bent over the toilet coughing and gagging, Cara was filled with joy. Was she going to be able to eat? Really eat?

She flushed the toilet and closed the lid, then washed her hands and rinsed out her mouth. Tillie was standing like a little ghost watching her.

"I'm okay now, babe, let's get some breakfast."

"I'm not hungry."

"You're not?"

"What's wrong with you? Are you going to die?"

"I'm not going to die, sweet girl. It's just side effects. They'll pass."

Ten percent, Cara's brain whispered, sending a cold chill down her spine. *Ten percent chance you'll die.*

"Your skin looks funny." Tillie pointed to Cara's arm. Cara looked in the mirror. Tillie was right. The skin on her arms were bagging down, making folds like wrinkled laundry, piled at her elbows and wrists. She wanted to lift up her shirt and look at her stomach, but resisted the urge.

"It's okay, they can fix that."

"How?"

"I don't know. It's time for breakfast."

Cara looked in the fridge for something to make for breakfast, but all she had was that horrible sawdust concoction and some Lunchables for Tillie. This was stupid. She could eat now, and she was going to eat.

"Let's run to the store, babe, I want to get a few things for breakfast."

"I'm still not hungry."

"Come anyway." It wasn't a question. Tillie nodded and went into her room to put her shoes on. Cara may have been pushing three hundred pounds, but she had raised a child who listened.

Headache mostly gone, stomach settled, the trip to the store was like she had been in prison her whole life and had finally been let out. She filled her cart, not with the ice cream and donuts and pizza she would have expected herself to buy, but with food, real food. Cream. Sausages. Pancake syrup. Foods that normal-weight people didn't think twice about eating, but had been forbidden for so long she couldn't remember what they tasted like.

Home, the smell of the cooking sausage brought tears to her eyes. Her mouth watered.

"We're having all of that?" Tillie said, watching her mother cook. Cara's heart sank to her feet. She had tried not to let her eating restrictions affect her daughter, but if pancakes and eggs and sausage felt like a feast to the little girl, she had failed.

"We are! Set the table, it's almost ready."

Tillie set the table. Cara saw her reading the nutrition facts on the syrup. She plucked the bottle out of her hands.

"Let's just eat, okay honey?"

Tillie nodded. "Okay, Mom. Let's eat."

Cara flipped a pancake onto her daughter's plate along with a hot sausage and some cheesy eggs and set it before her daughter, then made herself a plate. Tillie took a bite of the eggs.

"Mom, these are *good*!" Cara nodded and smiled. They *were* good.

They finished their breakfast together. Cara kept herself from licking her plate, but Tillie did not, and they both laughed.

Afterward, Cara started to wash the dishes. At first, she just felt a little faint. Then her head started swimming. She tried to back up into a chair, but she wasn't quick enough or coordinated enough, and she fell to the ground, her vision going black. Her head bounced when it hit the ground.

"Mommy!" she heard Tillie shout, and then she didn't hear anything else.

· · · • • • • • • · ·

She came to in the back of an ambulance. Tillie's scared little face was right by hers in the cramped space.

"Oh, baby, I'm so sorry," she said. "I'm sorry I scared you." She realized she was talking through an oxygen mask and reached up to move it aside, which was when she noticed she had IVs in both arms.

"What's going on?" she asked the young female paramedic.

"You seem to be severely dehydrated," the medic said. "Your daughter said you did some sort of weight loss shot?" She said it like it was something you'd buy at some shady gas station.

"Bentiga. It's FDA approved."

"Ah." The girl read a monitor, not making eye contact. She was skinny. She wouldn't understand.

"I'm fine," Cara said, struggling to sit up. She could see her feet past her stomach. She must still be losing. Good.

"Mom, you wouldn't wake up!" Tillie's voice rose in anger. "I called 911!" She started crying.

Cara felt awful. She hadn't thought about what she would be putting her daughter through. She had considered and dismissed the idea that she might die, but she hadn't thought about how bad the side effects would be, and what it would be like for Tillie to watch her go through them. She felt her own flare of anger, at the doctors and the nurses for not giving her more of a warning.

"Let me sit up!" she snapped at the paramedic.

The girl sighed. "We'll be at the hospital in a minute, then they'll get you in a bed and you can move around."

Tillie was still crying. Cara reached out and stroked her hair. "It's okay, sweetie. I'm okay; everything's going to be okay."

"You're not—" Tillie sniffled. "You're not okay. You're even skinnier than you were. Your skin looks super weird. You're sick."

"This is what the doctors wanted me to do. You know they've been telling me to lose weight? This is what's supposed to happen."

Tillie looked at her with eyes far older than an eight-year-old's. "I didn't mind that you were fat, promise. That kid at school is just a big bully. I'm sorry!"

Tillie had figured out that the final straw was the incident at the school, and blamed herself, Cara realized. Her stomach did a flip. If she died.... *No.* She wasn't going to die. Everything was going to be okay.

· · · · ● · ● · · · ·

Cara had been waiting for about an hour when a doctor finally appeared in her little bay. He flipped through her digital chart, swiping with his finger, then peered at her.

"Bentiga, huh?"

"Yes," Cara said, trying and failing not to feel attacked. Her whole life she had been told by doctors, by everyone, to lose weight. Now she was losing weight and everyone was questioning her.

"Well, what you're experiencing is normal for that medication. Once you are hydrated, there's not a lot else we can do. We just have to wait for the weight loss to stop. Or..."

"Or what?"

He paused. "Come back if you get below a hundred pounds."

Cara gulped. If she got below a hundred pounds, she'd be a walking skeleton. She thought of something. "How much do I have to lose for the skin removal?"

"You'll have to talk to your doctor about that. I'm not sure how much. A lot."

Cara didn't answer.

"Is my mom going to be okay?" Tillie asked the doctor.

He smiled at her. "Almost certainly," he said. "She's just going to look a little different, and she may not feel well sometimes."

"Wait a minute—sometimes?" Cara cut in. "These side effects pass, right?"

"Not all of them. You might continue to have migraines, and will almost certainly experience regular nausea and diarrhea. They didn't tell you that?"

Cara realized she hadn't asked. She hadn't asked nearly enough questions. She had just made herself chronically ill. For what? She looked at Tillie, who was on the verge of tears again. The little girl understood so much.

"Look at it this way; It's still an improvement," the doctor said, patting her foot through the blanket. He turned and left.

"I'm sorry, sweetie."

"I want to go home."

"Me, too."

It was thirty minutes before the next nurse came in, and Tillie didn't speak the whole time. Cara kept trying to get her to talk, but she just glared.

"We need to get your weight," the little nurse said when she did come in. "Do you think you can get up?"

"Yes, I think so."

"Here, I'll help you."

With the nurse's help, Cara made it to the scale, where she held her breath as the numbers ran. Finally, they stopped. Eighty pounds. She had lost eighty pounds.

"Congratulations!" the nurse chirped at her.

"Is it supposed to go this quickly?"

"How long has it been?"

"About twenty-four hours."

"Oh, my. Well, that's even better, then, right?"

"Right," Cara said, but her heart was beating hard.

The nurse followed her back to her bed. As she walked she felt her stomach flopping against the tops of her legs. Her gut had turned into a sagging flap of wrinkled flesh.

"I need to use the bathroom," she said.

"Of course, it's right over there." The nurse pointed. "I'll be back in a few minutes with your discharge papers.

In the bathroom, Cara looked at herself in the mirror. Most of the fat that had lined her cheeks and neck had melted off, leaving loose skin tinged a sickly gray color. Her eyes, she noticed, looked a little yellow. For the first time in years, she could see her cheekbones.

"I'm okay," she said to the woman in the mirror. "Everything's going to be okay. I can get the skin removal surgery, and then I'll be skinny, and it will all be worth it."

Discharge took forever, but finally it was time for Cara to get back into her clothes. She closed her eyes while she got dressed, something she had done for years now. Tillie stood outside of the bay. She still wasn't speaking to Cara.

Once she was dressed, Cara took Tillie firmly by the hand. She had summoned an Uber, and they found it quickly, right in front of the Emergency Room doors.

She got in, and she saw the driver's eyes widen momentarily when he looked at her, before he wiped his face back to neutral. Did she look that bad?

Tillie wasn't talking, but when Cara started to let go of her hand, the little girl held on tightly.

· · · ● ● · ● ● · · ·

It was a relief to drop Tillie off at school the next day. Cara had been trying not to let on how badly her head hurt. The child was upset enough already. But it felt like a knife was cutting into her brain.

By the time she pulled out of the school parking lot, she could barely see straight. She drove the route back home with one eye closed and the other squinted against the light. The other cars were just dark blobs. But she made it home. She took whatever headache medicine and pain killers that she could find and laid down on the couch, hoping to sleep off the migraine.

As she settled down, her skin pooled around her. She could see her hip bones cutting through her leggings, which she had safety-pinned to keep from falling down. But though the fat was gone, the stretched-out skin was not. As her head finally cleared, she decided to take a real look at her body. She went to the bathroom and did something she hadn't done since she was a teenager. She fully undressed and stood in front of the mirror.

She almost threw up. It was like she was wearing a monster suit. Her stomach stretched down to her knees. Her boobs, totally flat, hit her belly button. The skin on her arms folded down on itself and covered her elbows. She looked worse. So much wo rse.

Without even dressing, she grabbed her phone and dialed the doctor's office.

"How much weight?" she demanded of the person who answered the phone. "How much weight do I have to lose to get the skin surgery?"

"Hold on just a few moments, let me connect you to the nurse," the woman on the other end said professionally.

Cara waited, forcing herself to stay away from the mirror. She didn't want to see that again, but she was drawn to it, like picking at a sore. A deep, painful sore.

"This is Rachel," the nurse answered the line.

"It's Cara Berger. I need to know how much weight I have to lose before you'll remove the excess skin."

"How much have you lost?"

"It has to be a hundred pounds by now."

"What was your original weight?"

Cara told her.

"We'd like you to lose fifty percent."

"Fifty percent? Five-zero?"

"Yes ma'am."

"What if I don't?"

"If you don't, then you don't. It's still significant weight loss."

"I'm completely disfigured!"

"You wanted to lose weight."

"I didn't want this!"

"I'm sorry. You'll probably lose enough. A lot of people do."

"How many?"

The nurse paused. "Thirty percent."

"So seventy percent of people just live like this?"

"Sixty percent."

"What do you—? Oh." Ten percent died, Cara remembered. If it weren't for Tillie.... "I appreciate your time," she clipped out and hung up without waiting for the nurse to answer.

Cara stood in front of the mirror again, unable to help herself. She saw, reflected from the bathroom counter behind her, the scissors she used to cut Tillie's hair.

Without thinking, she picked them up and started cutting. After a few minutes, she realized she was going to bleed too much to finish the job, so she went to her office, still naked, trailing blood behind her, and got the stapler.

She cut and stapled, cut and stapled, until the job was done.

·········

Cara was cleaning the bathroom floor when the phone rang. She was on the last of the towels; the rest were soaked with her blood. She wiped her hands off on her pants as best she could and answered the phone. It was Tillie's school.

"Hi, this is Robin, the school nurse. Tillie is fine," the woman said as soon as Cara answered. Cara let out a sigh of relief.

"I wanted to get in touch because the students had a fitness activity in health class where they calculated their BMI, and Tillie has weighed in a little higher than we'd like."

A lead weight settled in Cara's stomach as the woman continued with the words she knew were next.

"We need to talk about diet and exercise."

Cara looked at the scissors sitting on the bathroom counter in a pool of blood.

"Yes," she said to the nurse. "Of course."

DEFECTIVE

ANKLES TO EARS, BROOKELYNN had been pushing for hours. She gripped the rails of the hospital bed and tried again to heave that which was inside of her out into the world.

"Come on, baby," she forced through gritted teeth with what breath she had left. "Let's GO."

Charles stood uselessly by. His soundtracks and massage balls and cool rags had gone by the wayside. This was raw, pelvis-breaking agony, and there was no help for it but for Brookelynn to get the baby out of her as quickly as possible.

A primal scream ripped from Brookelynn's throat as her vagina tore, top to bottom, straight down to her asshole. The pain was searing, burning, inescapable. There was nothing, nothing but pain.

"Push," the nurse told her.

"Push," the doctor told her.

"You can do it," Charles chimed in.

"Fuuuuuuck," she groaned. Some final thing broke inside of her and the baby slid out into the waiting doctor's hands.

She heard the woman gasp. It was not a good gasp, not a "this is the most beautiful baby I have ever seen" gasp. It was not an "oops" gasp, as though someone had forgotten the scissors to cut the umbilical cord.

Brookelynn's doctor had just made the sound every pregnant woman has nightmares about.

The baby cried, a hearty squalling sound, so the problem wasn't that the baby was dead. It sounded like a boy, angry at being thrust into the world as all newborns are. But that gasp. It worried her.

"Oh, God," Charles said. "Oh God, oh God." He stood staring. Gawking.

"What?" Brookelynn pushed herself up on the bed, put her naked legs back down where they went, prepared herself.

Whatever it is, it will be okay. I'm a mother now.

But there was no preparation that would have been enough for what she saw. The nurse laid the baby on her chest and she immediately wanted it off of her.

"I'm sorry," the nurse murmured. The doctor was silent, gathering herself together at the foot of the bed.

The baby rooted around on her with its approximation of a mouth and found her breast. Her whole body recoiled as it started slurping and sucking her nipple ineffectually, its sharp little tongue rounding on her sensitive flesh.

It was the single eye that was the worst. It had no eyelid. Its pupil was filmy and white.

The baby clung to her as she tried to keep herself from swatting it away, flinging it away. Its claw fingers clenched onto her skin, and it started screaming, frustrated and unable to nurse.

She had wanted a baby so much. She was forty, Charles only a year younger. They had been a childless couple for six years, and it was time to have a baby or just decide not to. So she'd thrown away her birth control and he'd quit smoking pot and they got pregnant.

They'd had routine ultrasounds and normal bloodwork and they'd never anticipated this.

It wasn't long before they were alone with the thing. The doctor had said that specialists would be by, but she said it with a sort of hopelessness.

The baby had been put in a bassinet, wrapped as much as possible in a regular swaddling blanket despite everything. It was crying.

The cry pulled at Brookelynn. It sounded like her baby. It sounded like a normal baby. But when she looked at it, bulging wrongly beneath the blanket, she just couldn't. Her stomach turned and she had tears in her eyes.

Charles was sitting in an armchair that was made to look comfortable but wasn't. He was staring at the baby.

"Should we try to hold it?" he ventured.

You're its mother! she told herself. *Hold your baby!* But she couldn't. She had to admit that she was repulsed by it, by its horrible eye, its puckered skin, its twisted limbs.

"You try," she told Charles.

Awkwardly and not able to hide the disgust on his face, he picked the baby up and held it crudely in his arms.

Brookelynn flashed to what it should have been like, the first time she saw her husband hold their child. She started to cry.

Her husband looked at her, tears running down his own face. As if to join them, the baby let up a yowl.

"I'm so sorry," Charles said, and put the baby back in the bassinet, flipping the blanket up over its face so they didn't have to see that staring eye.

The rest of the day was a blur. Brookelynn tried to eat but couldn't. The baby just kept crying. The nurses encouraged her to try to feed it, but even that was half-hearted, as though they knew they were telling her to do something impossible, something they wouldn't do themselves.

Eventually, a young nurse who had drawn the short straw came and tried to give the thing a bottle. It slurped and choked as the girl struggled to get it to eat. When the bottle was empty, its face, if it could be called a face, was covered in milk. But it was clear from the continuing hungry cry that the baby hadn't been able to drink.

Charles left. He said he was going to talk to the doctor, but he didn't come back for a long time and Brookelynn just sat in the bed letting the tears fall down her face, not even crying anymore so much as leaking sorrow.

She couldn't look at her baby. Couldn't bring herself to touch it. Couldn't stand to hear it.

She hit the call button.

The little nurse popped her head in a few minutes later.

"Can you take it away?"

"The policy is to have the baby in the room with mom for the first—" she looked at Brookelynn's face. "Yes. I'll take it—him. Sorry."

"Thank you."

After the baby was gone, Brookelynn managed to get a little sleep. Charles didn't come back. She woke, hoping that she had dreamed the nightmare, hoping that there was a smooth-cheeked baby with two blue eyes cooing in its little bassinet, waiting for her to hold him to her breast. But the room was empty.

She pushed herself painfully from the bed, her stitches pinching horribly, and clasped her gown around her backside. Finding her slippers, packed so thoughtfully in her go-bag, she shuffled down the hall, looking for the nursery.

She found it, and looked along the rows of perfect babies, swaddled carefully and cozily in their little blue and pink blankets. She prayed she would see a bassinet with her last name on it containing a tiny blue-blanketed baby that she could bring herself to touch.

Her child was there. He was as she remembered, worse in the bright white light of the nursery. It turned her stomach, but she forced herself to look at him.

I'm the mother, she told herself. *He has no other mother. It's up to me.*

As she watched, a nurse rounded among the babies, tucking a blanket more tightly around one here, replacing a pacifier there. When she got to Brookelynn's baby's crib, she paused. Gingerly, she pulled the blanket over his head, and then continued on. The baby wailed.

Brookelynn had been listening to the baby cry since she had pushed him out of her body, but something about watching him be left like that, hidden away and ignored, allowed his cry to finally pierce her heart. She realized, with finality, there would be nothing for this child but suffering. It was more than a birth defect, a shortened limb or a weakened heart, a cleft lip or an organ outside of the body. It was more than a twisted spine or blindness or deafness or a brain that would never function normally, more than oxygen deprivation or epilepsy or even bones that would break over and over. This baby, her baby, was horribly and wrongly made. An innocent, irrevocably broken before he had ever gotten a start.

She knocked on the locked door. The nurse answered, eyebrows raised.

"I'd like to take my baby back to our room, please."

"Name?"

"Church."

"Oh." The nurse couldn't help the quick look of abject pity she flashed toward Brookelynn before turning and grasping the cart holding her child.

Brookelynn took it from her.

"Thank you."

Not uncovering the face, she rolled the crying child back to her room. Charles was still gone. It was her job. She was the mother.

She pulled the blanket back and looked at him. It was so bad. That eye, that lidless eye, staring. That mouth. She shuddered, remembering when it had clamped onto her nipple.

"Daniel," she said to him softly, bringing herself to touch him gently, though it made her skin crawl. "Your name is Daniel."

She pulled a pillow from the bed and put it over his face, swift and firm but not so firm he would feel pain, only so that he would not be able to breathe. She tried not to wonder if a newborn could panic but couldn't help herself.

How long does it take for the brain to die? Surely for something with such tiny lungs, not long.

She waited until the baby stopped thrashing, then counted to a thousand.

Then she counted to a thousand again. Then again.

When Charles returned, carrying flowers and a car seat, she was still bent over the bassinet, counting. The baby was still, had been still for long minutes, but she held the pillow over his face, weeping.

Charles pulled her gently away.

"It's done," he said. "You did it."

"I'm sorry," she said.

"There was nothing else to do."

Colonoscopy

Note: The vast majority of colonoscopies are minor inconveniences with very few complications or side effects. Also, they can save your life. So please don't skip your colonoscopy.

They say the prep is the worst part. They're wrong.

When it goes down, it tastes like half-sweet motor oil, and you force it past the impulse to vomit into a stomach sloshing with more of the same. When it comes out the other end in its waterfall of shit and fluid, it has a very particular smell. A yellow smell. A clinging smell.

Eventually, all that's left is the slimy liquid rushing through you, for hours. It stings, because you've been shitting bloody diarrhea for weeks and your butt is completely raw from all of the wiping. At some point your asshole starts bleeding.

When you hobble—still squirting wet yellow farts and hoping your underwear can contain them—into the clinic, you can pick out which people among the scattered pairs have been flushed like a hose in the springtime. They're the ones that look like they'd be okay with dying.

The nurses make everything so comfortable when they take you back, tucking you under pristine sheets as though you aren't about to have a metal hose with a camera rammed so far up your anus that it wraps through you like a stiff snake, a yards-long metal curl, a cold cancer-finder.

You try to ignore the doctor spreading the cheeks of your white ass to access your anus. You try to forget that huge hemorrhoid you popped out in childbirth that never went away. You hope the last of the fluid isn't leaking out of you when they shove the thing inside. But you know it is, filling the procedure room with that sick yellow smell.

They say you don't remember anything.

But you watch the monitor as the camera spools through your large intestine. "What's that? What's that?" you ask, blurry but concerned.

"Give her more," the doctor barks at the anesthesiologist. Something is cranked and you wake up in the recovery room.

They say you come right out of sedation, no side effects, ready for the rest of your day.

You wake up with sharp abdominal pain, confused and crying. A woman you don't know takes you to a toilet and tells you to fart, but you can't, because trying to push the gas out is a new kind of hell. So you just cry. That's when you realize your lungs hurt, and your voice is gone, and they tell you that you had trouble with the sedation and they had to do something to your neck so you would breathe, that you'll be sore for a while. They have to tell you several times. You're still confused.

You just want to leave. As soon as you can stand up, you muscle your way into your clothes and your kind, patient husband helps you to the car. That's when you're supposed to go get a nice meal to reward yourself for your ordeal. But instead you're rasping that he needs to pull the car over now, *now*, and you're puking out the door with your head splitting, an ice pick through your skull and deep into your brain.

When they call, hours later, to make sure you're okay, you tell them about the migraine, and they tell you that's impossible, the sedation doesn't cause migraines. You hang up and put a fresh ice pack on your neck and lock yourself in a dark room and try not to cry again.

Eventually you manage some Ramen noodles. Eventually it's over, though your asshole is sore for a few days. Your hemorrhoid is inflamed.

You go in for a follow-up appointment, and they confirm what you already knew. Your disease has spread. You'll need an injection every two months. And another colonoscopy.

SIDE EFFECTS INCLUDE

LAURA POURED HERSELF A glass of wine—the good stuff, a red darker than blood.

"Can I get you a glass?" she asked her husband. Half-asleep in his recliner, he had apparently given up finding something to watch on Netflix and was scrolling through mindlessly, eyes almost closed.

He didn't answer.

"Scott!"

"Huh? No. Thanks," he muttered.

Laura remembered when they would drink two bottles of wine and wake up the next morning naked, the lube bottle empty and both of them feeling well-fucked but with very little memory of what had actually happened.

She tried again.

"I could call in to work tomorrow. We could sleep in?"

"I have to mow in the morning." He said it with a finality, one that made her feel like her vagina might as well be shriveled into nothing. Like she was never having sex again.

"Fine." She got up and, taking her wine, went to the bathroom, which is where she always went when she felt like she might cry and didn't want Scott to see her.

She leaned back on the sink and tried to remember the last time they had sex. It had been quick, her idea, and not that satisfying. She tried to get him interested in toys a few years ago, but he had been uncomfortable and a little grossed out, so she gave up.

She downed the rest of her wine. When her drink was gone, she opened the cupboard and popped an allergy pill out of its blister pack. If she couldn't have sex, at least she'd get a good night's sleep.

· · · · • • • • · · ·

Laura was a little fuzzy at work the next morning, but not bad. This was good, because as a 911 dispatcher she had to be reasonably sharp. Some days, when calls were slow, she felt like nodding off. But today had been busy with two nasty car wrecks, a domestic, and a few hallucinating drug addicts. She was exhausted by noon, so when Shirley stopped by her desk it was all she could do not to roll her eyes.

"Happy Saturday, right?" The woman's voice was grating. "I thought you might call in."

"Nope." Laura's voice was clipped.

"You have a reputation about Saturdays is all," Shirley continued, as though she were making pleasant conversation and not being a total bitch.

"Uh huh."

That line of conversation dying, Shirley tried another one.

"You know, they can do something about that hair loss," she said.

Laura looked at her. "What hair loss?"

"Oh, I'm sorry, you hadn't noticed? I hate to be the one to tell you, but you're developing a little...spot...up here." The woman gestured to the crown of Laura's head.

Against her will, Laura's hands shot up and searched the location, expecting to find nothing amiss and wanting to punch Shirley in the throat.

"Oh my God," she said as her fingers met smooth skin.

"You really didn't know? Well, gosh, I should have said something sooner." Shirley said, smiling broadly. She gave Laura a little pat, and Laura cringed. "I'm sure your doctor will have something. They gave my sister some wonderful drops. Didn't bring all the hair back, but it was better than nothing. At least you're blond."

Laura wasn't listening. She had grabbed her phone and was Googling female hair loss. What she found was not encouraging. Studiously, she ignored Shirley, who was still talking.

Finally, Laura looked up. "Don't you have something you need to be working on?"

"Me? Not really, my desk has been pretty slow today." Shirley patted her headset. Mercifully, though, a call must have come through, because she made a face and answered.

"911 what is your emergency?"

"Losing my fucking hair," Laura muttered, and turned away.

· · · · ● ● · · ● · · ·

"Would you be able to come in this afternoon?" the doctor's receptionist asked on Monday morning when Laura finally got through the unnecessarily long menu and reached a human. "We've had a cancellation at three o'clock."

Looking at her watch, she decided she'd just have time to make it across town after she clocked out.

"Yes, put me down for three, I'll be there."

"Got it! See you then."

Surely the doctor would have a solution, she told herself as she drove to the appointment a couple of hours later. Medical science could do damn near anything. Or maybe something with her diet...fish oil or some shit. She was too young to go bald.

A little voice told her, *You're really not. This is when it starts. Get ready.*

"Fuck that," she said, gunning her engine through a yellow light and swinging into the parking lot of her doctor's office.

When she went in, the receptionist smiled at her pleasantly and took her insurance card.

"Looks like your copay is seventy-five dollars," she chirped.

"Seventy-five? It's supposed to be forty."

The receptionist's brow furrowed as she peered at the screen. She looked up and shrugged a little.

"It looks like it must have changed. It says seventy-five. Do you want us to bill you?"

Laura didn't have seventy-five dollars. She had forty dollars she had transferred from her savings account, which was looking frustratingly thin. It pissed her off. She felt like at her age she should not be this close to broke.

"Yes. Please."

The woman smiled and gave her card back.

The wait was long. Laura half-watched the epic design battle taking place on the waiting room television while she counted the minutes ticking away on her watch. It was three-thirty by the time she was finally called.

She tried not to look when she was weighed, but as always she did, and as always she was horrified. How much more overweight was she going to get? One more fucking thing. Fat and bald. Great.

The nurse took her blood pressure, then started tapping away on the computer.

"What are we seeing you for today?"

Laura didn't want to repeat this to any more people than she had to, but she didn't see a way out.

"Hair loss."

"Is this new hair loss?"

"Yes. Very new."

Tap tap tap.

"Any recent changes we should know about? New allergies?"

"No."

"Any changes in your medication?"

Laura wasn't on any medication, other than Excedrin from time to time for migraines and the allergy pills to sleep.

"No."

"Okay, sweetie, hang tight and the doctor will be right in."

The doctor was not right in. The doctor was not in for another twenty minutes. Laura got tired of looking at her phone and crept over to the sink, forcing herself to look in the mirror. She hadn't done that yet, just felt the smooth skin and panicked but not brought herself to look.

She tipped her head forward and gasped. It wasn't a spot. It was a patch. A large, bare, shiny white patch, totally hairless. Right behind her hairline. How could she have not noticed?

The door opened behind her and she jumped.

Laura's doctor, whom she always tried to like but never quite succeeded, smiled thinly. She looked like she was annoyed at being awakened from an afternoon nap but had to be nice.

"I hear you are having some issues with hair loss," the doctor said without preamble. "Why don't you let me have a look?"

Laura, holding it together, got up on the exam table and took deep breaths while the doctor poked at her scalp. For a flash, she wished her husband were there, holding her hand, but she shook off the thought as silly. It was just hair. He was at work. Then that small voice again, *Would he even care?*

"Well, I do see some thinning typical of your age," the doctor reported. Laura's heart sank. "I can give you some drops to slow it down or even thicken it a little, but you should be prepared. Many women experience some level of baldness as they age."

"I'm only forty!"

"Are you still having periods?"

"Yes!"

"I'd anticipate that will stop fairly soon now. Come back in six months and we'll evaluate you for hormone replacement."

The doctor smiled her thin smile and left.

· · • • • • • • · ·

As soon as she left the doctor's office, Laura went straight to the pharmacy and waited while her prescription was filled. She took the crisp white bag as though it were contraband and rushed home, imagining strands of her hair falling behind her along the way, littering the roadway like lost years.

When she got home, she saw her husband's truck wasn't in the driveway. She wondered where he was. Usually on days he mowed he spent the whole damn day in the yard, futzing around.

A little relieved to be alone, she hurried to the bathroom and locked the door. Opening the package, she fumbled out the bottle of drops. Not bothering to read the directions or warnings, she liberally applied the drops to her head and slathered them around.

"This better fucking work," she said. She stared for a bit while it soaked in and then, feeling stupid for expecting an immediate result, went to her room and searched for a baseball hat in the mounds of old clothes at the back of her closet.

She came across a red Cardinals cap. Tears came to her eyes when she remembered going to the game with Scott. He'd gotten one of those huge beers and they'd sipped it together, giggling. So long ago.

Cramming the cap on her head, she headed to the kitchen and started washing dishes, trying not to think of her balding head, distant husband, or shitty job. But there was nothing else to think about, and her tears mixed with the water as she scrubbed the dishes clean.

· · · ● ● · ● ● · ·

Laura's head was itching. Then it was burning. She told herself it was because the drops must be working, but realized she knew nothing about the side effects. And maybe she had used too much.

She dried off her hands and went to the bathroom to take a look. When she pulled the cap off, it came away sticky.

Her head was covered in blisters. Huge, watery, bulbous blisters as though she had been burned. A few had popped and were seeping blood-tinged pus down her scalp. Her skin was mottled and angry, not just where she had put the drops, but all over. She reached up and touched her head and her hand came away wet, with strands of hair sticking to it.

The rest of her hair was falling out.

The back door closed quietly, and Laura heard her husband moving around in the kitchen. Part of her wanted to stuff the cap back on her ruined head and pretend nothing was wrong, but a deeper part of her wanted him to see it and still love her, comfort her, help her find a solution.

She walked into the kitchen, hands at her sides, tears in her eyes.

"Hi honey," he said, his head in the fridge.

"Scott."

"Hm?"

"Scott."

He looked up, a slightly annoyed expression on his face. "Yeah?"

"My hair. My head."

His eyebrows raised and his eyes focused on her, finally.

"Looks like you have a little rash there, honey. Maybe you should see your doctor." He turned his attention back to the contents of the refrigerator.

Laura's heart sank. He didn't care.

"Where have you been?" She was angry and wanted a reason to lash out that was not her own crisis.

"I went to lunch with a friend from work."

An alarm bell went off in Laura's head. Scott never met up with co-workers on the weekend.

"Until five o'clock?"

"It was a late lunch, ran over."

"Then why are you looking for food in the fridge?"

He pulled back and shut the door, stiffening.

"What are you asking me?"

She was being paranoid, she told herself. She was upset.

"Nothing. I'm going to urgent care about my head." She half-hoped he would offer to come along, show some scant interest in what was happening to her.

"Okay," he said. "The co-pay is like a hundred and fifty bucks. Do we have it?"

"No," she said, and left.

· · · · • • · · · ·

Laura could tell the young doctor was grossed out by her head. Doctors were supposed to be unfazed by bodily issues, but this one must have selected the wrong field. The woman put on two pairs of gloves before examining her.

The blisters burst at the slightest touch, spurting liquid in unpredictable directions. The doctor kept her mouth firmly closed.

Laura tried not to whimper as the exam went on.

By this time, nearly all of Laura's hair had fallen out. It was clumped wetly on the back of her shirt and littered the exam table.

"Well, this is an unusual reaction to the drops, but it is included in the list of possible side effects. Still, we need to take a biopsy," the nurse said, breathing through her mouth. The sores had developed a smell. "I'll put in the lab order."

"There's nothing you can do now? For the pain?"

"I can prescribe something, yes. Traladon should do it."

"Are there side effects?"

"Drowsiness, dizziness, weakness, nothing serious that won't go away."

"Are you sure?"

"Don't worry. We'll get you taken care of."

"Will my hair grow back?"

"If not, there are some really great wigs available these days."

· · · · ● · · · · ·

The biopsy was excruciating. Laura made the mistake of going straight to the lab instead of picking up the pain medicine first.

The tech scraped at her weeping, disintegrating scalp until she felt like nothing was left. Soon she was bleeding freely.

"Please stop!"

"I'm sorry," the older woman said, scraping away. "I'm almost done."

The only mercy was that she gave Laura a little plastic cap before she left. It kept the bloody ooze from getting in her eyes and ears. She had soaked a sleeve trying to keep her face clear.

Laura picked up the pain medicine through the pharmacy drive-through and took two right away in the car with no water, then drove home half-blind with pain and let herself in.

Scott was in his chair, TV on, dozing.

She didn't bother waking him, instead making herself a cup of chamomile tea with milk and heading to her rocking chair in the front room, hoping she could find some calm as the pain medicine kicked in.

Suddenly, she felt dizzy. So dizzy. Holding onto the wall, she managed to make it to her bedroom and crawl under the covers. The room spun around her, around and around. She leaned over the edge of the bed and vomited violently. It went on and on.

"Scott," she moaned finally when she caught her breath between waves. The living room was right off the bedroom. She heard him shuffle in his chair and fart. "Scott!"

"Huh? Yeah?"

"I need help."

He appeared in the doorway, bulky in his sweats. "What's up?"

"I'm sick. They gave me—" she threw up all over the floor again, the vomit spattering back up in her face. It took her a full minute to catch her breath. "They gave me Traladon."

"Why?"

Seriously?

"My head. I need you to take me to the hospital."

"Um, okay. Let me get dressed."

She puked again.

"You're dressed! Help me!"

He sighed. "Okay, sorry." He looked at the sea of vomit that had spread over the bedroom floor and was clearly at a loss.

"Come around the other side!"

"Should I...should I get a bag or something? Are you going to keep puking?"

"I don't know! Just help me!" She fell back, exhausted, on the pillow. He went to the kitchen and came back a few moments later with a white trash bag, which he handed her, then stood back and waited.

She reached out both her hands for him, and he hesitated a moment too long to disguise his disgust. Finally, he pulled her from the bed. Her cap slid off of her head.

"Oh, my God!" he exclaimed, flinching back.

"Please, just take me to the hospital," she cried.

Scott looked around as though hoping for help, but seeing none, he got a determined look on his face and pulled her to her feet.

Laura was so dizzy she couldn't stand. He placed her arm around his shoulder and hauled her to his truck. She didn't have the strength to pull herself up so he had to lift her, his facial expression set and long-suffering, his nose pointed as far away from her as he could manage. As he lifted her, she remembered when he carried her over the threshold of their home. It hurt more than any exploding blister.

· · · · ● · ● · · · ·

At the emergency room, the triage nurse took a look at her bag of puke and suppurating scalp and got a wheelchair to take her back.

"You can come too," she told Scott, but he shook his head.

"I'll wait out here, thanks."

The nurse gave him a look and helped Laura into the wheelchair.

She was given a new puke bag, which she promptly used. The nurse helped her into a bed and took her history.

Laura wished Scott had followed her back, but realized he probably wouldn't be able to answer most of the questions. When had he last remembered her birthday, even?

Repeating back her history, the nurse clarified: "You were experiencing hair loss, so you got some drops from your doctor, which caused these...blisters. Then you took pain medicine for the blisters and began to experience dizziness and vomiting. Is that right?"

Laura nodded, trying not to puke.

"Okay. Do you have any other concerns?"

Laura shook her head. She had so many concerns, but nothing this woman could help with.

"The doctor will be here momentarily. Hopefully we'll get you feeling better soon."

Laura waited for an untold amount of time before the doctor came in. He was a handsome man about her husband's age but with light still in his eyes. He asked her the same questions the nurse had, then said, "We're going to start you on some intravenous anti-nausea medication and a gentler pain killer. That should help quite a bit."

"Is there anything we can do about my head?"

"You say you got a biopsy today? We'll check on it. Likely, you're going to have to wait for it to heal."

He smiled kindly and Laura tried to smile back but threw up instead, gagging and heaving out the tiny amount of stomach acid left in her. It burned. When she was done, the doctor was gone and the nurse was attaching bags of fluid to an IV pole, preparing to jab her.

"Are there any side effects to these medicines?" Laura was hoarse.

"Nothing common," the nurse answered. "Some potential for heart issues, but your chart doesn't show any history of heart problems?" Laura shook her head. "Other than that, just some rare cases of swelling. If that happens, we'll stop the medicine right away and try something else. The most likely thing is that you'll stop throwing up and feel better."

Laura held out her arm. The nurse slid the needle beneath the skin. The tell-tale blot of blood didn't hop into the chamber of the needle. She had missed the vein.

"Well dang it, sweetie, I guess we're going to have to hunt a bit. You're dehydrated."

Laura bit her lip as the nurse moved the needle beneath her skin, probing and pushing it this way and that as she tried to strike a vein.

"It keeps rolling on me." The woman had a look of frustration on her face as she pulled the needle out. "Let's try the other arm."

The other side was the same as the first, and by the time the nurse found the vein there were tears streaming down Laura's face.

"Sorry about that, darlin'. We'll get some fluids and medicine in you now. You'll feel a lot better soon."

The woman left Laura alone.

She wanted her mother. Her husband was fucking useless. If her mom had been alive, she would be right there, holding Laura's hand, asking a million questions, getting in the way. Caring. But she died just last year, and now there was no one.

Her stomach beginning to settle, Laura laid her head back and tried to sleep.

· · · · ● · ● · · · ·

She felt it in her tongue first. And then her ankles. A fullness. A tightness. Her throat. She panicked.

The scream she let out was strangled by the swelling in her throat and mouth, but it was enough to bring a nurse to her side.

"Uh oh, sweetie, looks like we have some swelling!" the nurse said, lifting the head of her bed and finding an oxygen mask, then popping out of the bay to say with far greater urgency, "We need Dr. Stacks stat."

Laura felt her eyes squeeze shut and reached up to her face. Her eyelids were swollen to the size of lemons and getting bigger.

"Husband," she choked out into the mask. "Scott."

"Try not to talk, the doctor is on his way."

Laura pulled the mask from her face. "Need my husband," she coughed.

The nurse squeezed her balloon-sized hand. "I'll send someone to the waiting room to get him."

The doctor arrived.

"Bentonyl," he said to the nurse. "Now."

"Right away." Laura heard the nurse's footsteps patter away, then return. Laura felt her next to the bed, hanging a new IV bag.

Laura heard herself wheezing as she struggled to draw in a breath. And then no more wheezing. Her throat had closed.

She thrashed on the bed, fighting against the suffocation.

"Where's her husband?" she heard the doctor say.

"We couldn't find him."

"Try again."

She saw black.

· · · · ● · ● · · ·

When Laura came to, she was in a new room. Her throat hurt terribly. She reached toward the pain, but someone caught her hand.

"No, no, let's not touch."

She found she couldn't speak.

"We had to do a temporary tracheostomy," the nurse said. "Now that your airway has opened up, we'll be taking it back out, but it's going to take us a little bit to schedule the decannulation. In the meantime, you just need to rest."

Her eyes fell on the nurse and she gasped, the air rushing in through the tube in her throat and burning down her raw windpipe to her lungs.

The nurse had no face. Her face had been removed. All that was left was shining muscle over bone and burst blood vessels. The woman's muscles moved into the shape of a smile.

"Are you comfortable?"

Laura twisted and thrashed to her feet, trying to run. The IV pole clattered to the ground behind her. She ripped the IV out of her arm with a spurt of fluid and stumbled past the nurse, out the open door of her room.

The hall was full of people whose faces had been somehow cut off. Their ears hung unsupported, their scalps slid back, revealing skull. The floor was slippery with their blood.

"Ms. Niemer!" She heard the nurse's voice behind her. "You're okay, it's okay! You need to come back!" She kept going.

Moments later, there was a page for security to come to the ICU.

She scrambled down the hall, searching for stairs or an elevator. She found the bank of elevators and frantically jammed buttons, but when the door opened, two tall men in uniforms walked out. The skin of their faces was sliding down the front of their uniforms and their teeth grinned at her behind glistening muscles.

"Ma'am, we're going to need you to calm down," the burlier of the two guards said in a calm voice, as though he wasn't missing his face.

"Stay away from me!" she tried to shout, but it just came out as a whoosh of air through the tube in her throat. She ran the opposite direction, but they chased her and one of the men grabbed her, putting her into a hold so she couldn't escape. Her limbs were pinned. She was voiceless. She could smell the coppery tang of blood from his ruined face.

The other man came up beside her and gave her a shot in the arm. Moments later, she slumped in the burly guard's arms, unable to move. Unable to fight. Unable to scream.

·········

She was conscious as they lifted her to a gurney, conscious as they wheeled her back to her bed, conscious as they attached restraints to her arms and legs.

The doctor was there. He also had no face. Laura, drugged and limp but still panicking beneath the paralysis, watched his mouth move.

"Hallucination?" he asked the nurse, who was starting a new IV, this time in her neck.

"It seems that way. With her not being able to speak, it's hard to be sure. But she looked like she was seeing something that frightened her."

"Let's get her on a short-term dose of Thronomine. Any history of mental illness?"

"Not in her chart."

"Check with her primary care doctor before administering."

"Will do."

The team turned and looked at her in the bed. The rest of their skin seemed to be separating from their body and slipping off onto the floor.

The doctor reached out and touched her foot with his bleeding hand.

"Don't worry, Ms. Niemer. You'll feel better soon."

The doctor and nurse both left.

Laura lay staring at the ceiling, wondering where her husband was. Wondering what the next side effect would be.

·········

Laura needed to leave. She needed to get out. It was like a motor was inside of her, turned up to ten. She could not stay still in this bed any longer, could not stay in this hospital any longer. Her arms and legs jerked against the restraints.

She couldn't speak, so she banged with her fists and kicked until someone came. It was a nursing assistant, who looked at her from the door with wide eyes. Her face was intact.

Laura imagined how she must look to the girl. Her head, covered in leaking pustules. A tube jutting from her bloody neck. An IV leading to her jugular vein. Strapped down, jerking uncontrollably. No wonder the aide was afraid.

Trying to hold her limbs still, Laura lifted a still-spasming arm toward the girl, hoping to make it clear that she wanted the restraint removed.

"I'm sorry," the aide whispered, and skittered away.

Laying helpless and twitching in a hospital bed, Laura was completely helpless.

A nurse approached the room and popped her head in.

"It looks like you may have started some dyskinesia from the Thronomine. I'll let the doctor know and he'll probably discontinue."

Laura tried to nod.

"Are you still seeing things?" The nurse moved closer, tentatively.

Laura shook her head as best she could.

"Okay." She watched Laura struggle for a moment. "I'm going to remove these restraints to allow you to move a little more freely. I know this must be uncomfortable."

Once the bonds were removed, Laura felt some relief from the feeling of needing to flee. Her arms and legs, however, continued twitching.

They continued twitching even after the medication was removed.

She tried to hug them to her body, but they kept flailing. For hours.

The doctor came back. He, too, had a face now, one with a deep worry line between his eyebrows. He looked her in the eye when he talked to her.

"This side effect of Thronomine is called tardis diskinesia. It...can be permanent. So we need to treat it. However, the medication used for this, Aureno, has some significant risks of suicidality."

Did she hear him right? They were going to give her something that made her want to kill herself?

"We need your consent before we continue."

He tried to hand her a form, but her flailing arm knocked it back. The nurse took it from him and brought up the meal tray, laying the paper on its sturdy surface. The doctor handed her the pen, which she helped Laura grasp.

Permanent? If this continues, I'll want to kill myself anyway.

She signed, a haphazard scrawl that covered half the page.

The medication was administered through an injection. It burned. Laura felt like she was drowning in a sea of pain. The IV in her neck hurt every time she moved. The tracheostomy ached deeply. Her head was still seeping bloody pus. She didn't dare to ask for pain medication because of the possible side effects.

So she suffered.

· · · · ●· ●· · · ·

Laura was in the hospital for three days. Scott stopped by once, on the second day. In a hurry.

He didn't touch her. Dumped a bag of clothes in a chair and asked hushed questions of the nurse.

Laura overheard him ask how much "this" was going to cost. If she could have spoken, she would have demanded a divorce. She wanted to kill him.

He left after twenty minutes, a disgusted look on his face.

Her jerking limbs slowly relaxed. But her head did not heal. The blisters kept forming and breaking, forming and breaking. They changed the bandages, sometimes hourly, and they were always soaked.

Once she could hold still to write, they gave her a dry erase board and a marker.

"When can you remove the trach?" was the first thing she wrote.

The nurse called the doctor. He told her that there may have been damage to her windpipe that would require it to be in longer. He ordered imaging. It was inconclusive.

· · · · ● · ● · · · ·

On day three, she felt a compulsion.

It wasn't the first time in Laura's life that she had been suicidal. College had been hell, and when she had her miscarriage, she sat in her bathtub with a bald razor more than once.

This felt different. This felt like certainty. Like a relief, an escape. She was voiceless, ugly, helpless, sick, alone.

She began to plan.

The next time the nurse checked on her, she had a note ready.

"I want to go home."

The nurse tucked Laura's blankets a little tighter around her. "You need to be cleared by your doctors. I'll let them know."

Dr. Stack cautioned her that she would need to take care of her trach tube—a horrible process involving suction and mucus. She nodded, trying to show that she was ready and capable. He asked if she had a caregiver at home.

"My husband," she wrote. The doctor wanted to talk with him, give him pamphlets, directions. But, in the end, he signed her release.

Then she had to meet with the psych guy.

"Are you having any thoughts of harming yourself?" he asked, as though he were asking about whether she had a stomach ache.

Her mind conjured up an image of herself with her head in the oven and a lighter in her hand. Of the bottle of painkillers leftover from her root canal, empty. Of the garage, and her car running. Her husband's gun, fallen to the floor in a pool of blood.

She shook her head, no.

In the end, he signed the paper too.

The nurse helped her dress and offered to call her husband for her. Laura declined.

"Uber?" she wrote on her board. The nurse nodded and made the call.

When she was wheeled out of the hospital to the waiting car, prescriptions piled in her lap, Laura felt nothing. She felt like she was already dead.

On the ride home, she watched out the window. Everything was a shade of gray. There was no color. She saw a couple in the car next to hers, laughing, happy. It seemed strange and unusual. Why would anyone laugh? At any moment, they could discover something horrible, a bald patch, a weird lump, and then life would be only suffering until they died.

The Uber pulled up in front of her house. There was an extra car in the driveway.

··•••·••••··

They were in the bedroom, fucking. Loudly.

Laura walked back outside, to her husband's truck. The idiot's door was unlocked, and the gun was in the glovebox, loaded.

Picking it up, she appreciated the weight of the weapon in her hand. She flipped off the safety and went inside, walking in the open door to her bedroom. She no longer wanted to die. Not yet.

Her husband's bare, pimply ass was in the air, someone's skinny legs wrapped around his waist. They didn't see her.

Pulling the trigger felt good, so she did it again and again. The naked bodies jumped and tore and collapsed. Her husband and his fuck buddy bled

together, on her flowery sheets. They screamed and
writhed, then stilled, then died.

Laura tossed the gun on the bed with them.

She went to the bathroom and looked in the
mirror. She was spattered with blood. A little
blond fuzz had sprung up on her head over the past
few days, unnoticed.

Her eyes fell on her trach tube.

The doctor had said that if the tube accidentally
got dislodged, she was not to panic and to call 911.
That it was survivable. That it was likely they'd be
removing it in a week or so anyway.

Why wait?

Unbuckling the collar that held the device tight,
Laura grasped the plastic shield on either side, and
pulled. The tube slid out of her throat like a tape-
worm, clinging a little and then releasing.

At first, she couldn't catch her breath. She
gasped and air escaped out the hole in her neck. She
clutched her hand to the hole and blocked the air,
then found herself able to breathe. A little blood
eked out from beneath her hand. The pain was

immense, but by now Laura was used to pain. She forced herself to breathe deeply.

After a few moments, the bleeding stopped. She pushed the hole in her throat tight and covered it with a large band-aid, then tried breathing through her nose. No air leaked this time.

She washed her hands. She washed her face and head, removing the layer of gunk from the now-healing blisters and the flecks of blood from the shooting. She dried her hands and face on a clean, fluffy towel.

Laura went to the kitchen and poured herself a glass of dark red wine. A merlot, just the right amount of dry.

Her stomach growled. Now that she had decided to live, she was incredibly hungry.

She found a knife and went to the bedroom, where the naked bodies were cooling. The knife was nice and sharp. Her husband's skin stuck a little around his lips as she removed it, but a sharp tug did the trick. Peeling it the rest of the way, she dropped the skin in a little heap, then moved on to the woman. It was no one she knew.

After the woman's skin was off, she positioned the two bodies facing each other, a pair of lovers staring into one another's lidless eyes. That made her smile.

When she was done, Laura carried their faces into the kitchen. She found the board that she and Scott had been given as a wedding present—by his uncle, if she remembered right—and sliced the meat into little bite-sized strips. She artfully arranged the meat along with a handful of cheese cubes and some crackers, then found an apple that wasn't too soft and sliced it up too.

She poured herself another glass of wine, and ate it all.

It was delicious.

Sixteen

"Jeannie, can you *please* get off that thing and clean your room?"

No response.

"Jeannie," Mick said, more loudly but trying not to yell. "Get off that thing and clean your room."

Jeannie plucked a headphone out of her ear and glared at her father. "I'm busy. We're in a match."

"You're always in a match," Mick said, gripping the door frame of his daughter's room and holding onto his temper. "Your room is dirty."

"So *you* clean it." Jeannie said, putting the ear bud back in her ear and refocusing on her screen.

She's a teenager, she's a teenager, she's a teenager, Mick told himself, taking deep breaths. *They're all like this.* But he knew it wasn't true. His friend Chris's son was a helpful, respectful young man. Took out the trash without being asked. Said please and thank you.

But he loved his daughter, so he wasn't going to say the things that were going through his head. It was those damn friends of hers. They were all a bunch of little shits. That witch Corrina...he wished his daughter had never met her. Before they met, Jeannie had been a nice kid. A little sassy, but fundamentally kind. And then when Pam died, it was like the rest of her softness was gone. He didn't know where his little girl had gone.

If Jeannie's mom were still alive...no. He wasn't going to go down that path today. It was too hot to be miserable, too. *Let it go,* he told himself. *Just let it go. A messy room is not that big of a deal.*

"Dad, can we for the love of God turn the thermostat down?" Jeannie said without looking at him. "It's hot as balls in here."

Mick cringed at his daughter's language. So crude. He didn't care if she cussed with her friends—all kids did that—but cussing in front of him felt so disrespectful. He didn't answer her, but he went to the thermostat to check the temperature. It was set to 76. *I guess I could turn it down a little*, he thought and hit the button. The screen flashed for a second, then went blank. The overhead light blinked off. Panic jumped in his gut, started coursing through his bloodstream. He tasted the metal of adrenaline. If the air didn't work...his condition...*oh no.*

"DAAAAD." Jeannie called from her room. "The wifi is down!"

"I know—it's the power," he said, but he said it quietly, trying to fight his panic.

"DAD! I said the wifi is down!"

He didn't answer. The generator...he had to get the generator going. Pam was the one who knew how to work it, but she had shown him once and he would figure it out. It was hooked directly into the HVAC, so it should cool the house down pretty quickly. Would it be quickly enough? He felt like he might throw up as sweat poured down his forehead.

"For God's sake, Dad, are you just ignoring me?" Jeannie had emerged from her room and was standing, hands on hips, still in her pajamas.

"The power's out," he said, brushing past her on his way outside, to where the generator sat. His hope.

"So what are we going to do about the wifi?" she yelled after him. He shut the door behind him.

The heat hit him like he had stepped into an oven. So hot. Scary hot. His skin softened and his sweat thickened. He would have to hurry. They had talked about getting a battery backup, but Pam had always taken care of those things and she had gotten sick before she got around to it.

Mick's hands shook as he primed the generator. He held his breath as he pulled the cord. It sputtered, then nothing. He pulled again, harder, faster. Not even a grumble this time. The sun glared down on his head. The cacti behind the house stood silent, watching him struggle. The air shimmered with the heat. His scalp burned, d ripped.

Mick realized that in his hurry he hadn't checked if the generator had fuel, and he looked at the gauge. It was empty. He ran for the door, wracking his brain for where Pam had stashed the extra gas. His legs felt like jelly. He pushed himself to hurry.

As he passed through the living room on his way to the utility closet, he saw that Jeannie was at the modem, plugging it in and unplugging it. He had told her the power was out, but she was still trying. His heart ached that what she was most worried about was the damn wifi. She knew about his condition. She should be with him, frantic with him, searching for gas and pulling the cord for the generator while he hid from the sun inside. She was old enough—sixteen. But all she knew how to do was look at those goddamn screens. He pushed the hurt feelings away and opened the door to the utility closet. The strong scent of gas hit his nostrils. A scary thought crossed his mind, but he rummaged through the bottled water and old roller skates. There, the gas can. *Thank God.* He picked it up.

"FUCK!" he said aloud. It was empty, completely empty. His fear was validated. It must have all leaked out, hence the strong smell. He scrambled through the rest of the junk in the closet, but it was the only gas can.

"Dad, can you call the power company or something?"

"They won't be here soon enough," he said.

"Soon enough for what?"

Surely she hadn't forgotten. She had been young when it had almost happened the last time, but he knew that they had talked to her about it, how dangerous the heat could be for him. They didn't go outside, didn't ride ATVs in the desert like their friends, or go for hikes to see the majestic red rock formations. They just hid, from the heat, from the sun.

"I won't make it that long, we have to figure out something now."

"What the hell are you talking about?"

"My condition?"

"Your—" Her eyes widened. She must have remembered. "Shit. Dad."

He could feel the skin on his arms turning beginning to drip.

"Yeah. Shit."

"What are you going to do?"

"I don't know."

"Don't we have some fans somewhere?"

Mick's heart jumped. "Oh my God, you're right. Do you know where they are?"

Jeannie thought. "The attic?"

"I can't go up there," Mick said.

"Fine, I'll go."

"Okay. Thank you." He felt tears welling in his eyes.

Jeannie headed for Mick's bedroom, where the pull-down staircase for the attic was. "Duh," she said over her shoulder.

Mick stood at the bottom of the stairs. The heat wafted down, a dense and dark heat. He started to step away, as quickly as he could, but it was too late. His leg melted under him and he fell with a squishing sound to the ground.

"Jeannie, hurry!" he choked out before his lips melted off of his face. Once it started happening, it was fast. All he could think about was Pam. If she had been there, this would never have happened. He was almost angry with her, for getting sick, for dying. Now their daughter would have to see him...like this. Would have to watch him die.

His mind flashed back to when Jeannie was a little girl, before he had developed his condition and they would play in the yard outside in the summer. He'd spray her with the hose and she would run through the stream of water, screaming with joy as the dirt turned to mud and coated her little feet. Then she'd chase him with her wet hands and he'd pretend to be afraid of her, running and screaming himself.

At the foot of the attic stairs, Mick's skin turned wet. His bones became slush.

"Okay, I found them...." Jeannie was backing down the stairs, her hands full with two oscillating fans. She stepped off the stairs and her foot hit the liquid seeping across the hardwood floor.

Mick's eyeballs floated in the goo his body had become. Jeannie watched as they too dissolved.

"Well, fuck," she said softly. "Fuckity fuck fuck." She stepped gingerly out of the puddle and wiped her feet on the hand-made rug that lay on the floor next to the bed. She set the fans on the bed.

The puddle was blocking the door.

"How am I going to get out of here?" she mused to herself. She pulled her phone out of her back pocket.

Corrina! she texted. *You are never going to believe what happened.* She held her breath, but the message went through. "Yes, I still have data!" she said quietly.

Omg, what happened???

My parental unit bloody MELTED.

Come again?

Ikr, he melted.

Corrina just sent a series of question marks. Jeannie aimed her phone at her father's puddle and snapped a picture, then sent it.

You're freaking serious!?! Corrina wrote back immediately. *You have to put this on Tik Tok.*

You're a genius! I didn't even think of that. But anyway, do you have power?? It's hot as a witch's taint here and the wifi is down.

Yeah, do you need us to pick you up?

You are an excellent friend.

Be there in a bit.

Jeannie closed the message window and studied her father. She noticed something gold floating in the puddle. It was his wedding ring.

Gingerly, she bent over and picked it up, wiped it off, and put it in her pocket.

"Guess I'll have to jump," she sighed to herself. She backed away and gave herself a running start.

THE VISITOR

by Rik Hoskin

ADAM MCCALLUM WATCHED IN awe as the elderly woman selected two apples from the supermarket display. Her movements were slow and deliberate, her forehead creased in concentration. She reminded him of his mother, and watching her pack the apples into her basket beside her other groceries made Adam think of the wonderful apple pies she used to make. He could almost taste them now, their rich combination of sweet and sharpness. It must be almost forty years since he had sat at the old kitchen table in Birch Street and tasted his Mom's apple pie. And yet, as he watched the frail old woman choose her apples from the pallet, he could taste that pie like he'd only just finished it, topped off with a scoop of ice cream. He pushed the thought aside and went back to his cup of coffee.

The coffee in this place was lousy, but it was convenient to where his last fare had left him, stranded out here over the river with almost no chance of picking up another fare that might take him back into the city and towards his apartment. He could work the suburbs for a couple of hours now that he was here, but he hated the suburbs with all their little one-way streets and hidden turnings. The last time he had enjoyed traveling through the suburbs he'd been twelve years old astride his bicycle. Could go anywhere on a bicycle, not like today in his silver people carrier with all the street signs and their no entries and their no stopping *at any time* and their handicapped users only. It was getting so a guy couldn't earn an honest buck no more. He'd drink the coffee, then head back home. He'd been driving the cab for almost fourteen hours now and the coffee was the only thing keeping him awake. Home was sounding pretty good.

He took a sip and almost gagged. "The hell is this?" he muttered before taking a second, tentative sip. He could remember when a guy could order coffee and they would know what you were talking about. These days, it was all you could do to get them to hold back on drowning it in a quart of milk and frothing the thing up until it looked like some damn kids' shake.

Maybe, he thought bleakly, *I can move my mother to a smaller room.*

···•••••···

Back at his apartment, the answer machine was flashing three messages. He let them play as he sat in the armchair, pattern almost gone from the headrest.

"Hi Adam, it's me," a familiar woman's voice began after he'd suffered a computer telling him that he had won a vacation to Florida. "It's Alice. Can you please call me? It's important." She gave her number and added another "please" before hanging up. She sounded worried, he thought as he hit erase. This woman had been phoning him, off and on, twice weekly for the last nine months, and he had no idea who she was. They had spoken a few times, early on, when she had caught him at the apartment, and she'd said something about being his sister. Adam was an only child, and he had told her that repeatedly; she had the wrong guy. He blamed that fad for family research--all these stay-at-home moms with too much time, trying to prove they were distantly related to Washington or Lincoln or the King of England.

He was too old to have a stalker. Alice sounded like a nice enough lady but, well, he was 58 years old, widowed, and holding down two jobs just so he could keep his mother at a decent standard of care in the hospital. He didn't have time for crazy broads who thought they had some special connection to him. "Go stalk a movie star," he told the answer machine.

The final message was from his office, reminding him that he needed to be in early on Monday because they had a big client coming over. *Sure,* he thought. *When would I have time to take a vacation in Florida?*

· · • • · • • • · ·

The beige paint of his mother's hospital room was cracking, he noticed as he arrived for his seven PM visitor slot. *Wonder if they'd let me patch that up, maybe take a little off the bill.*

His mother lay dozing in the bed. She looked so fragile to Adam, her thin arms like a sparrow's bones, likely snapped by nothing more than a hard look. He watched her shallow breathing. Beside the bed, a pump extracted the mucus that had gradually overwhelmed her lungs over the years, gurgling and groaning like a hurt animal, and a heart rate monitor chirped happily to itself, a metronome timing his mother's remaining life. Ticking down her remaining days, like some mechanical Grim Reaper constantly checking his watch.

He brushed the loose white strands of her hair from her forehead, feeling her clammy sweat. She didn't notice. No doubt she had been sedated by Doctor Amara again--he had told Adam this allowed his mother a chance to recover, but Adam secretly suspected it was a way to keep her quiet for the nursing staff who tended to her around the clock. Not that he had seen his mother make much noise in the last eight or nine months. The most she had done was wheezed, and occasionally blinked heavily in recognition of her only son during one of his visits.

He sat down in the chair and watched his mother sleep, that incessant tick-tick-tick of artificial life going over and over. She really did look like that woman in the supermarket, the one with the apples. His mind was playing tricks on him, of course, but he couldn't stop thinking about that woman and how much she looked like the woman in the bed.

They took good care of his mother here, feeding her by hand when she would accept it and by drips when she couldn't, rolling her to ensure she didn't get bedsores, attending to her needs, both medical and mental. They had supplied a television set, built into a frame on the ceiling, so that she could watch if she felt up to it. The television screen, Adam recognized dismally, was bigger than the one in his own apartment. They had also supplied a large electric fan--another expense on his bill, whether his mom used it or not.

Perhaps she won't mind if I get her a smaller room, Adam thought. *Maybe in a cheaper facility. Because this place is crippling me with their fees, raising this and that charge, adding up heating and lighting and breathing costs on top of everything.* This place would see him in a grave before his mother, the way they were pumping him dry.

Maybe they'd let him paint the walls and give him some kind of discount on his fees for a while. Maybe they'd give him a regular job painting up the whole place even, and he could quit running the taxi in the evenings. That would mean spending even more time in the hospital though, and he hated the place.

He had been here once himself, as a patient, for an operation. A minor thing--appendix or in-grown toenail or something. So minor, in fact, he couldn't even remember what it had been. He laughed as he sat there, chortling at the memory of no memory at all. So unimportant he had pushed it from his mind.

A light knock at the open door brought him out of his reverie. A nurse--Hispanic looking and pretty, the one he thought of as "Maria" in his mind even though he was pretty sure that wasn't her name--knocked again until he looked up.

"Five minutes, Mister McCallum," she told him with her apologetic smile.

"How's she been? I ain't had time to see her in a few days and I wondered if there was any change in her, y'know, condition."

Maria showed her pristine, white teeth again as she offered another sympathetic smile. "You should talk to Doctor Amara about that," she said, "but, between you and me, your mother's been no trouble at all. Her breathing seems to be getting a little stronger, and she's been waking up in the afternoons."

He nodded thoughtfully. "That's good," he agreed. "Maybe ... I dunno, maybe you could think about releasing her."

"I don't think that would work right now, Mister McCallum. She needs constant--24 hour--care."

He nodded, resigned. *And in the meantime*, he thought, *I'm working my fingers to the bone to pay for it.*

Maria checked the watch attached to her tunic. "Four minutes until visiting hour ends."

"Thanks," he said. "Hey," he added, gesturing around the room, "who does your paint work here? The walls and that? Is it a firm, do you know?"

······ ·· ·· ·

Adam was checking the double entry books he was responsible for at the office when his telephone extension rang. He reached across, picking up the phone. "Adam McCallum," he said.

"Adam, it's Alice"--the familiar voice again. "I left a message for you, but you never called me back," she babbled on, the words coming out in a frantic rush. She sounded hysterical.

When she finally paused for breath, Adam spoke into the receiver. "Listen, lady. I don't know how you got this number, but I don't want you calling me at work."

"But, we really need to talk," Alice began.

"Yeah, you need to talk. You need to talk to a damn head shrinker," he said angrily. "You're a nut, lady. Leave me alone."

Alice was sobbing. Her voice came out in fits and starts, like a stalling motor car. "Please, please, Adam. Don't be like this. Please. Just talk to me. I won't call you at work again. I'm sorry. Please. Can we just meet? Can I see you, face-to-face?" The question hung, as tears broke into her voice.

Adam took a steadying breath, standing up and gripping the edge of the desk with his free hand. "No," he told her firmly. "I don't want to meet you. I don't want to talk to you. Don't call me here. Don't call me at home. Don't call me, peri-od."

He slammed the handset down and glared at it for half a minute.

Bob Kent, sitting at the next desk, peered his head over the low wall that separated their cubicles. "Everything okay?"

Adam shook his head, still glaring at the phone. "Damn nuts," he replied. He felt his heart pounding hard in his chest.

"You look kinda rattled," Bob told him. "Why don't you take the afternoon off?"

Adam shook his head. He couldn't afford to take the afternoon off, not with his mother in the hospital. "I'll be fine," he told Bob, heading to the rest room. Once there, he splashed cold water on his face, and looked up into his eyes in the mirror. He was looking old.

"Damn crazy broads," he muttered as he watched the water flow out of the basin.

· · • • • • • • · ·

The rain was belting down. Adam listened to the water as it beat against the roof of his people carrier in the taxi rank outside the station. He watched the sudden flow of people exit the station with the arrival of the 10.30 from the city. They pulled their coats close against the cold winter night, reaching for umbrellas or pulling a newspaper or magazine over their heads as they made the frantic dash to the bus stop. It was late now, and these people were the theater crowd, shift workers and hotel staff. In another thirty minutes it would be the bars turning out, tobacco-scented coats stinking up his cab. He preferred the theater people--they were inevitably couples or foursomes, eyes shining with the production they had just seen, full of smart conversation. Sometimes they'd get into his cab and start singing arias from some opera he'd never seen, or maybe fluffing through the words to one of the musicals. He'd drum his fingers on the steering wheel, mouthing the words he knew.

Adam heard someone pop open the door behind him. Checking his mirror, he saw a small, elderly woman ducking into the cab, a fur trimmed hat on her head. He slipped into gear as she gave him an address. He knew the apartments she wanted, they were only three blocks away.

"You're out late," he said, by way of conversation.

"Well, you get the work where you can," she told him.

He glanced at her in the mirror again, and something flickered at the back of his mind, a note of recognition. "Where do you work?" he asked, trying to remember where he'd seen her before, peering at the dimly lit, back seats in the reflection.

She enunciated her words with relish. "Anywhere I can," she told him. "I tread the boards. Not so many parts for an actress of my vintage, of course."

"Actress?" he muttered. She was familiar, but the hat obscured so much of her face it was hard to tell. "Would I have seen you in anything?"

She shrugged. "Possibly. Do you attend the theater often?"

"Not really," he told her. "More of a TV man. Sports mostly. Do any adverts?"

"If only," she responded. "That's a tidy income if you can secure it. Most of my work is corporate. It's for a very small client base, and I don't often get to play to real audiences. I only got the part tonight because the regular actress was ill. Can you believe it? An understudy--at my age!" She laughed.

McCallum pulled the people carrier close to the doors of her apartment building. "This okay?" he asked.

She reached into a small, leather purse, leant forward, and thrusted the money at him through the gap in the safety partition. As she did so, he got a better look at her in the mirror.

It was the woman he had seen at the supermarket. That supermarket was only four streets over--little wonder she shopped there. As he watched her, he felt his stomach churn. She looked so much like his dying mother, he realized. Almost identical.

Her voice broke into his thoughts, asking if he wanted the money or not, and he apologized as he took it. "Sorry, you just remind me very much of someone I know," he told her.

In response she reached for her throat, looking a little self-conscious. He watched in the mirror as she stroked a charm on a necklace she wore there--a letter B, wrought in gold. It was an unconscious reaction on her part, a sign of her nervousness.

He watched her walk to the double doors of the apartment building, her frail frame struggling against the wind, the rainwater splashing around her, and he thought--*she's just like her. If my mother were walking around, physically capable, this woman could be her. If she weren't in the hospital, suffering from ... her condition. Suffering from ...* And he stopped then, trying to recall what it was his mother was in hospital with. He knew the word for it, he was sure. It was there, on the tip of his tongue. But, no matter how hard he tried, the word, the disease, the illness, wouldn't come to mind. *Strange*, he thought, *I spend so much time visiting her and I can't remember what it is that's wrong with her.* He sat in his cab at the roadside a long while, trying to remember the name of the illness.

· · · · ●· ●· · · ·

On Wednesday evening, Adam's mother was snuffling in what appeared to be a restless sleep when he entered her room. He watched her quietly from the doorway for several minutes, afraid to disturb her. As he watched, he thought of the elderly woman he'd driven home a couple of nights before. They were incredibly similar, he concluded, and he felt sad. An aimless kind of sadness, like he had been defeated from within.

Doctor Amara, his mother's primary physician, was passing down the corridor when Adam spotted him. "Doctor Amara, can I have a word?"

Amara looked at him over the rims of his spectacles, smiling his ingratiating smile, teeth brilliant against his tanned skin. In another life, McCallum thought, Amara could have been a movie idol; he had the looks. "Mister McCallum," Amara said in his rich, warm voice. "What can I do for you today?"

Adam scratched his head, trying to form his question into words. "It's about my mother," he said slowly, and Amara nodded.

Amara closed the door and looked at Adam with a concerned frown. "What's on your mind?"

Adam felt foolish, but he had come this far so he had to ask the question now. "This is going to sound stupid, I know, but I was wondering ... what is it that my mother is suffering from? I seem to have forgotten."

Amara smiled reassuringly, nodding his head. "You have a lot on your mind. It is understandable that a detail might slip away from you now and then." He placed a firm hand on Adam's shoulder. "It's really nothing to get worked up over."

Adam nodded, feeling better already.

"We are doing everything we possibly can," Amara continued, "to ease your mother's condition. *Nth stage cancer*, Mister McCallum. All we can really do is make her comfortable, you understand?"

He nodded, relieved. "You're doing a bang-up job, I know, doc. All of you. That pretty nurse. She's great. You all are. I'm sorry. I've not been sleeping so good. Strange phone calls and long hours and, well, I don't gotta tell a doctor about long hours, I guess."

Amara laughed politely. Adam thanked him for his time, and watched as the doctor departed.

When Doctor Amara was out of sight, Adam quietly pushed the door closed and sat at his mother's side in the chair. He wanted so much to cry, he felt so foolish. How could he forget his mother's sickness? How could he forget something so crucial to his life? He bit on his knuckles, holding back the tears he could feel welling. Amara must think he was a terrible son. To forget why your mother is in the hospital. It beggared belief. He was probably telling the nurses right now, and they would look at Adam and view him as a callous man once they knew. He wouldn't blame them. How could he have forgotten?

He looked up at the sleeping figure, her shallow breaths in unison with the bleeping monitor at her side. He shouldn't have asked. There must have been some other way to find out what it was that his mother was here for, rather than embarrass himself like that. At the end of the bed was his mother's chart. Could have just looked at that, he thought, berating himself.

Adam reached for the chart. It was in a little blue folder made of thin, cheap card.

LYNNE McCALLUM (f)

it read in bold type on the front of the file.

Adam flipped it open, gazed at the selection of graphs and charts that made up the nine loose pages of material therein. On the final page was a small section of text, with next of kin (himself) and other details of family and address.

He didn't recognize the address. With a start, he re-read the address that was listed for his mother, and realized that he *really* did not know it. He was a cab driver, and he thought that he knew the city and its suburbs well, but this address was nowhere he had ever heard of. Not his mother's, not anywhere he knew.

He removed the page from the file, held it under the lamp to see if maybe he'd misread it somehow. With the lamp on it, Adam could see a further notation on the reverse side of the sheet, bleeding through with the light. He flipped it over, and saw a hand-written note in blue ink, the characters wide and curved, slanting across the otherwise blank sheet:

BEATRICE NEELY

Who is Beatrice Neely? Adam asked himself. Next to the mysterious name was an eight digit number, and Adam recognized it as a phone number in the suburbs somewhere, south of the river. Still clutching the sheet of paper, Adam walked out and headed for the payphone at the far end of the corridor, marching swiftly in determination.

A teenage girl--a patient of the hospital--was chatting on the payphone when he reached it, loudly chewing gum as she spoke to her mother in a resigned, disinterested voice. Eventually, after a torrent of sighs, the girl finally hung up. She shrugged at him apologetically. "She's not even my real mom," she said to him as if that explained everything.

He nodded in response. "I think I know what you mean," he said, looking at the phone number on the piece of paper.

Adam dialed the phone number. It took him two tries to get it right, his hands were shaking so much. After three rings a machine picked up, and a well-spoken woman's voice came over the connection. "Hello, you've reached Bea Neely, but I'm not here right now. Please leave a message at the beep or, if it's about an assignment, either call my agent or call me direct on my mobile." She proceeded to give her cellphone number, repeating it to be sure. On the second read through, McCallum took down the number on the back of the sheet he'd taken from his mother's file.

Then, carefully, he dialed the second number--Beatrice Neely's mobile. It took a few moments to connect, and then he listened to it ring for a second. As soon as it started ringing he pulled the receiver away from his ear and held his hand over the earpiece, muffling its report and listening to the noises of the hospital around him. Barely, he could make out the sound of a phone ringing at the other end of the corridor. He let go of the receiver, leaving it dangling on the end of its steel coiled wire, and rushed back to his mother's private room.

As he reached the door of his mother's room, the ringing stopped, but he knew it had come from within. His mother remained lying in the bed, asleep and oblivious to everything that had happened. "Beatrice Neely," he said as he entered the room, but the woman in the bed did not stir.

In fifteen minutes, he realized as he checked the face of his watch, *my visiting hour will be over. I won't be able to come again until Saturday, and if I'm cabbing then I won't even be able to make that.*

· · · · • • • · · ·

Ten minutes later, the nurse--Maria--poked her head around the door and saw Adam McCallum dozing by his mother's side. "You have five minutes, Mister McCallum."

He looked up at her, eyes bloodshot and bleary, as if he had been crying. In his hands, she noticed, he held a sheet of paper and a small plastic object--a cellphone. "Are you ... is everything okay, Mister McCallum?" she asked politely.

"Can I show you something?" he asked, and she approached without thinking anything of it. She stood by his chair as he turned over the piece of paper in his hands. She saw the blue ink scrawl, recognizing her own handwriting. "Who is Beatrice Neely?" he asked.

She shook her head, smiling in uncomfortable denial. "I don't think I can ... I mean ... that is to say, you should really discuss this with the doctor. If you want, I can ..."

He turned on her then, and she saw the anger in his eyes. "Screw Doctor Amara. You tell me what's going on," he growled.

She turned, taking a stride towards the door, but Adam grabbed her wrist with a powerful hand, dropping the sheet of paper to the floor. Maria spun around and looked at him, terrified. "I don't know," she babbled. "I don't know. Please let me go, M-m-mister McCallum. Please, I don't know anything."

He pulled her close then, and bellowed his question in her face. "What don't you know?"

And then she let out an ear-splitting scream. Adam let go of her wrist, shocked at the sudden shriek, and Maria dashed out the door, her low, white heels clacking against the vinyl tiles.

A few seconds later, four people stood in the open doorway to the room--Doctor Amara, two nurses and one of the hospital porters. The hospital porter could be trouble, Adam realized.

Amara held his hands up, speaking softly to Adam, maintaining eye contact throughout. "Okay, now, Mister McCallum. Just calm down. We're all friends here. No one is going to hurt you. You know that. Just calm down."

"I trusted you, doc," Adam told him, his voice low and menacing, "so I'm going to trust you now."

"That's good," Amara told him, taking a step closer.

"So, tell me," he said, "who is Beatrice Neely and where the hell is my mother?"

"Your mother is in the bed, right there, Mister McCallum," Amara said, gesturing behind Adam.

"Yeah," he replied. "That's what I thought, too. I look at this old lady and I think she's mine, my flesh and blood. But she ain't, is she?"

Amara looked apologetic and the nurses looked uncomfortable as they watched from the doorway behind the burly porter. Maria had joined them now, her face pale, her eyes red with tears. "Please, Mister McCallum," Amara began. "You're clearly under a lot of pressure and ..."

Adam launched himself at the doctor, coming in low, sweeping his legs out from under him. In a second, Amara was lying flat on his back and Adam swung punch after punch into his face, bloodying his nose and lips. "Just tell me who she is!" he howled, punctuating each syllable with another hard jab of his fists.

Finally, the hospital porter grabbed Adam from behind, pulling his arms to his sides in a bear hug, yanking the flailing man from the doctor's form. "Come on, sir," the porter's deep voice boomed at Adam, but Adam heard it as though through the water of a swimming pool, distant and muffled. The blood was pumping in his ears with loud, pounding hammer blows, a blacksmith working at his anvil.

Elsewhere, one of the nurses was calling for security, and another tentatively edged into his field of vision: Maria, he recognized as he struggled in the vice-like grip. In her hands, Maria held a hypodermic syringe.

Seconds later, a sharp pain went though Adam's upper arm, and he watched as his vision seemed to cloud over. *I guess it's going to rain*, he thought, as he descended into blackness.

· · · ● · ● · · · ·

Adam woke up in a windowless room that smelt of disinfectant, and his head felt incredibly heavy. The light that came from an overhead bulb seemed exceptionally bright to his eyes, and he blinked it back several times before warily opening his eyes fully.

A voice from somewhere in the distance said, "He's awake." It was a man's voice.

Adam looked around, trying to see who else was in the room. His head didn't want to co-operate for a moment, and lolled heavily on his neck until he finally raised it. Three men in white lab coats were huddled by a bank of computers, looking across at him. A wave of nausea hit him as he raised his body, and he slumped back into the chair. "What's going on?" he asked, bewildered.

A familiar face stepped under the light. Adam looked up at the handsome features of Doctor Amara. "Hello, Mister McCallum," he said. "You've calmed down now." Amara had a band-aid across his nose, and his face was grazed and swollen. The beginning of a black eye was forming a ring on the left hand side of his face, and his spectacle lens was cracked.

"I remember," Adam began, trying to piece together what had happened, "hitting you. And a woman's name. Beatrice. Beatrice Neely."

"Yes," Amara explained, "a fine, talented actress. We've had her on contract here at the hospital for several years now. Something about her elicits sympathy in our," he pondered the final word a moment, "clientele."

Adam's head was pounding. "My mother," he stated, unsure of how to phrase the thought.

"Yes," Amara agreed. "Your mother."

"What happened?" Adam asked slowly, feeling the pieces floating around in his mind.

"Your mother died years ago, Mister McCallum," Amara stated. "But when you came to us for a minor operation, nine months ago, we did a little extra surgery, so that she might live again. In a sense."

"I was here?" Adam asked, confused. "Nine months ago? I don't remember what ... what it was."

"Appendicitis. Quite unusual in a man of your age. Still, you signed the release forms and we did the operation and it was a marvelous success. You've not had any trouble with it since, have you?"

"Not that I can recall."

"You see, Mister McCallum," Amara continued, "hospitals are a business. We've got to make a profit, just like everyone else. When Beatrice told us that you'd picked her up in your taxi earlier this week, we realized that it might affect the conditioning." He gave Adam a long, hard stare. "But, we can fix that."

"I don't understand," Adam admitted.

"Beatrice is the dying mother for a lot of our clients, Mister McCallum. She comes here, eight hours a day, and remains fitfully asleep while a whole platoon of doting relatives come and keep her company, each allocated a little shift so that they'll never meet." Amara smiled as he continued. "And each of you happily pays out for that marvelous room, for the big television and the extra fans and lights and everything else you're told she needs, because none of you would want your mother to suffer unduly. And, you all assure yourselves, she'll be dead soon so it's better to spend a little extra now to keep her comfortable because it won't be forever."

"I do two jobs to pay for that room," Adam grumbled.

"And you get what you pay for," Amara said.

"How did you ...?" Adam began, confused.

"When you were here for your appendix, we did a little extra work, implanting new memories over your old ones. Altering your family life, your recollections of your mother and your upbringing. If I remember correctly, you had a sister originally but we couldn't incorporate her without major work, so she had to be dropped. Beatrice became your mother, and you love her dearly and would do anything to ease her suffering."

"You crook bastard," Adam spat at him, lunging out of the chair. He collapsed to the floor as his weakened legs gave out from under him.

"Not really," Amara told him. "You see, you signed the release forms, Mister McCallum. What we did was perfectly legal."

"Legal, maybe, but immoral as all hell," Adam muttered, trying to get up off the floor. It felt like he was trying to get up off the depths of the ocean.

Amara looked down at the pathetic figure on the floor. "It's just business, Mister McCallum. We've got to turn a profit like everyone else. And it made you happy, to care. Pretty soon, you won't remember any of this anyway, so I wouldn't worry about it now if I were you." Amara rubbed his jaw and winced. "You know, perhaps this time we could use Rose Whitbourn as the mother figure," he mused.

Amara smiled as the assistants lifted Adam from the floor. "You'll like Rosie--she's quite demanding, and she has a very large, exclusive room with a breathtaking view over the city. Really quite magnificent."

ABOUT RUTH ANNA EVANS

Ruth Anna Evans is a horror writer, anthologist, and cover designer who lives in the heart of all that is sinister: the American Midwest. She has been composing prose of all types since childhood but finds something truly delightful in putting her nightmares on the page. She has self-published the horror collection *No One Can Help You: Tales of Lost Children and Other Nightmares*, along with novellas, novelettes, and several short stories. She is the editor of *Ooze: Little Bursts of Body Horror*. She also has work appearing in *Dark Town*, an anthology from D&T Publishing, *We're Here* from Gloom House Publishing, and *The First Five Minutes of the Apocalypse* from Hungry Shadow Press. She is the author of *What Did Not Die,* published by PsychoToxin Press, and the upcoming novella *Do Not Go In That House* from Gloom House Publishing.

Follow Ruth Anna on Twitter @ruthannaevans and on Facebook at Ruth Anna Evans. Her website is www.ruthannaevans.com.

ALSO BY RUTH ANNA EVANS

ABOUT RIK HOSKIN

Rik Hoskin is a multi-award winning writer of novels, graphic novels, video games and animation. He won the Dragon Award for Best Graphic Novel for White Sand (with Brandon Sanderson), which also made the New York Times Bestseller list. He writes SF novels under his own name and as "James Axler", and has written horror short stories for various publications including Cosmic Horror Monthly and Cornice. He also writes video games, where he has served as head writer, and has written animation for BBC television in the UK. His most recent project is the new Wheel of Time comic book adaptation based on Robert Jordan's novels.

ALSO BY RIK HOSKIN

<u>Short Stories</u>

Inferno (Games Workshop)

Cosmic Horror Monthly

Cosmorama

Cornice

Pyre Magazine

COVER DESIGN BY RUTH ANNA EVANS

For more information about custom cover design and premade covers, visit ruthannaevans.com.

Printed in Great Britain
by Amazon

36185989R00098